Limpy has a vision. A world where cane toads and humans play mudslides together. And help each other with the shopping. And share their slug sauce and maggot moisturiser.

But how does a young cane toad discover the ancient secret of living in peace with humans? First he has to dodge the killer trucks and supermarket trolleys. Then he has to stop his cousin declaring war on the entire human race.

Oh, and he has to take a trip to the Amazon.

The uplifting tale of one cane toad's heroic journey (with his sister and cousin) across oceans, continents and some really busy roads.

Also by Morris Gleitzman

MORRIS GLEITZMAN

TOAD AWAY

Puffin Books

Puffin Books

Published by the Penguin Group (Australia)
250 Camberwell Road
Camberwell, Victoria 3124, Australia
Penguin Books Ltd
80 Strand, London WC2R ORL, England
Penguin Putnam Inc.
375 Hudson Street, New York, New York 10014, USA
Penguin Books, a division of Pearson Canada
10 Alcorn Avenue, Toronto, Ontario, Canada, M4V 3B2
Penguin Books (N.Z.) Ltd
Cnr Rosedale and Airborne Roads, Albany, Auckland, New Zealand
Penguin Books (South Africa) (Pty) Ltd
24 Sturdee Avenue, Rosebank, Johannesburg 2196, South Africa
Penguin Books India (P) Ltd
11, Community Centre, Panchsheel Park, New Delhi, 110 017, India

First published by Penguin Books Australia,
a division of Pearson Australia Group Pty Ltd, 2003

1 3 5 7 9 10 8 6 4 2

Text copyright © Creative Input Pty Ltd, 2003
Illustrations copyright © Rod Clement, 2003

The moral right of the author and illustrator has been asserted

Typeset in 13/15pt Minion by Midland Typesetters, Maryborough, Victoria
Printed and bound in Australia by McPherson's Printing Group,
Maryborough, Victoria

National Library of Australia
Cataloguing-in-Publication data:

Gleitzman, Morris, 1953– .
Toad away.

ISBN 0 14 330047 4

1. Bufo marinus – Juvenile fiction. I. Title.

A823.3

www.puffin.com.au

For
Melanie
and
Nick

1

'Stack me,' said Limpy. 'This is my lucky day.'

He hopped closer through the long grass for a better squiz.

There were three of them. Big ones. Fully-grown, by the look of it.

Perfect, thought Limpy.

He had to admit they were magnificent creatures.

Their picnic rug was pretty nice too.

'They're called humans,' said a grasshopper. 'You can tell from their smooth skin and fat bottoms and unwise choice of shorts. I'd watch out. They hate you dopey cane toads even more than runny poo.'

'I know,' said Limpy quietly.

He tried not to be scared.

This was the chance he'd been looking for. Three humans relaxing on a picnic. Three humans exactly where he wanted them.

'Sorry, Uncle Ian,' whispered Limpy. 'I'll have to put you down. I can't tackle these humans with a dead rellie on my back.'

Limpy slid Uncle Ian off his shoulders and laid him on a soft patch of moss. He knew what he was about to do was very dangerous, but the sight of Uncle Ian's poor flat body, criss-crossed with tyre tracks and baked hard in the sun, made something inside Limpy harden too.

With determination.

Limpy thought of all the other poor rellies he'd seen squashed by humans on the highway. All those poor startled eyes glaring out of flat tummies and poor tragic ears poking out of even flatter bottoms.

'Those humans over there are so busy eating,' he whispered to Uncle Ian, 'they won't notice me. I can creep up and get really close without them seeing me, and then I can . . .'

'Stab them with their own cutlery,' said the grasshopper. 'In the buttocks.'

Limpy looked at the grasshopper, shocked.

'I'm not going to stab them,' said Limpy. 'I'm going to make friends with them.'

The grasshopper stared back, looking just as shocked.

'Make friends with humans?' it said. 'Why would you want to do that? Specially hairy ones with tattoos and big boots.'

'If I can make friends with them, this won't

happen any more,' said Limpy, pointing to poor flat Uncle Ian. 'Friends respect each other. They don't bash each other with rocks and drive over each other in vehicles.'

The grasshopper snorted. 'You haven't seen humans after a few beers.'

Limpy sighed.

'Aunty Pru reckons friendship is possible between all species,' he said. 'Except the ones that eat each other. Humans and cane toads don't eat each other, so we can be friends if we want to.'

'Yeah,' said the grasshopper. 'And sludge worms might fly.'

Limpy decided to ignore the grasshopper.

If I'm going to pay those humans a social call, he thought, I should take them a gift. Something nice for their picnic.

He peered over at the men. He could see pies in their fists, and sausage rolls in their lunchboxes, but no sauce.

Perfect, thought Limpy. I'll whip them up a batch of Mum's slug sauce. That'll get the friendship off to a great start.

While Limpy rummaged through the stinkweed looking for slugs, he had a wonderful vision of humans and cane toads being the best of friends. Going on bush walks together. Playing mudslides. Swapping recipes.

He plucked a fat slug off a stalk.

'Ow,' said a muffled voice.

3

At first Limpy thought it was the slug.

'Do you mind,' said the muffled voice.

Then Limpy recognised the complaining tone.

Goliath.

Limpy looked around, but couldn't see his cousin anywhere.

'You're standing on him,' said the slug.

Limpy looked down. Under his feet was a big clump of stinkweed.

'Get off,' said the stinkweed.

Limpy hopped back, startled.

The stinkweed rose slowly into the air. Under it, glaring at Limpy from a bog hole, was a familiar warty face.

'Goliath,' said Limpy. 'What are you doing?'

Goliath clambered out of the hole, the stinkweed still on his head.

'At the moment,' said Goliath, 'I'm getting a headache.'

'Sorry,' murmured Limpy.

He saw there was mud all over Goliath's big body and face. Usually when Goliath had mud on him it was in splotches. This was different.

'That mud,' said Limpy. 'Why's it in wavy lines?'

'Commando camouflage,' said Goliath.

Limpy was impressed. Usually when Goliath played commandos he made do with swamp slime on his face and a sprig of wattle in his bottom. These wavy lines must have taken ages.

'I'm on a military operation,' said Goliath.

There was something in Goliath's growl that made Limpy's warts start to prickle with concern.

'Goliath,' said Limpy. 'I'm in the middle of something pretty important myself. Would you mind playing your commando game somewhere else?'

'It's not a game,' said Goliath, glaring at the men on the picnic rug and flexing his poison glands. 'I've declared war on humans.'

Limpy stared at him, horrified.

Goliath gripped a sharp stick between his teeth, threw himself on the ground and started wriggling on his stomach through the long grass towards the humans.

Limpy flung himself after Goliath, grabbing onto one of his cousin's big feet. For a while he was dragged along behind Goliath, grass stems jabbing him under the arms.

Then Goliath stopped.

'Limpy,' he said. 'Let go and that's an order. I can't go into battle with you hanging off my foot. It's not good for your crook leg.'

Limpy clung on tight.

'I know how you feel, Goliath,' he said. 'But war isn't the answer.'

'Yes it is,' said Goliath, glaring over at the picnickers. 'Let's see how humans like having *their* brains poking out of *their* ears and wee coming out of *their* noses.'

Limpy let go of Goliath's foot and grabbed one of his big brawny legs. He knew that beneath

Goliath's tough scowling mud-streaked exterior, in among the half-chewed swamp rats and car accessories, lay a gentle heart.

'War will just make things worse,' said Limpy. 'Sorry, haven't got time to chat,' said Goliath, pulling his leg away. 'Got a battle plan to follow. Fourteen hundred hours, attack humans, kick their buckets of chips over, stab them in the shins with sharp bits of pie crust.'

'The buttocks,' said the grasshopper. 'Hurts more.'

Limpy realised one of Goliath's fists was buzzing.

Goliath opened it. A cluster of dazed bush flies sat on his palm.

'Aerial attack force, prepare for action,' commanded Goliath.

The flies looked unhappy.

'You can't send us over there without artillery support,' said one. 'Those humans might have insect spray.'

'Be quiet,' roared Goliath. 'You're in the military now.'

'Sorry, sir,' muttered the fly.

'You two,' said Goliath to the grasshopper and the slug. 'Form a platoon and prepare to follow me into battle.'

'Yes, sir,' said the slug. 'Does this mean I'm relieved from sauce duty, sir?'

'Silence in the ranks,' said Goliath. 'Stand by to attack.'

Stack me, thought Limpy. This is worse than I thought.

He had a horrible vision of Goliath starting a huge war and being crushed by a human tank, or even a human lunchbox. And then Mum and Dad and Charm and cane toads everywhere being wiped out.

'Goliath,' he said. 'Listen. Let's try my way first.'

Goliath looked at him thoughtfully. 'What, you mean jump on the enemy out of trees and stuff swamp slime up their nostrils?'

'Not exactly,' said Limpy. 'I mean try and make friends with them.'

Goliath's eyes bulged so much that for a moment Limpy thought Goliath was going to explode and spray warts in all directions.

'Make friends with them?' croaked Goliath. 'Are you mad?'

'Got it in one,' muttered the grasshopper.

Goliath snatched up poor flat sunbaked Uncle Ian and waved him under Limpy's nose.

'You can't make friends with monsters who do this,' yelled Goliath. 'All you can do is try and wipe them out, or at the very least force them back to the carparks they came from. And that's what I'm going to do.'

Limpy tried to stay calm. He loved Goliath very much, but sometimes, he thought, Goliath is like one of those forms of swamp life that are so stupid they don't even know when a lizard is eating their brains.

Perhaps it's not so bad, Limpy told himself. Perhaps Goliath will come to his senses and realise he's not going to win a war with an attack force of one cane toad and a few insects.

'Actually,' said the slug to Goliath. 'Those three humans look pretty tough. I don't think we'll be able to wipe them out on our own.'

Limpy, relieved, could see that Goliath was thinking the same thing.

Goliath glared at the slug.

'Leave the military planning to me, private,' he said. 'We won't have to wipe them out on our own because I've got an army.'

Limpy's throat sac bulged with alarm.

'An army?' he croaked. 'What army?'

'I'll show you my army on one condition,' said Goliath. 'No blabbing about it to the enemy.'

Limpy sighed.

'Goliath,' he said. 'Humans won't want to be friends with us if you keep calling them the enemy.'

But Goliath wasn't listening. He was hopping away down a bush track.

Limpy struggled to keep up. He wished he had big muscly legs like Goliath. He also wished his crook leg didn't make him hop in circles. But most of all he wished his dopey cousin wasn't putting all cane toads everywhere in serious danger.

A hopeful thought struck Limpy. Perhaps the army was only in Goliath's imagination, like the self-peeling snails Goliath daydreamed about quite often.

'Atten-shun!'

Limpy jumped, startled. Then he realised it was

Goliath's voice, booming from the other side of a clump of bushes.

Perhaps Goliath's just yelling at some grasshoppers he's eaten, thought Limpy even more hopefully. Telling them not to jump around so much in his tummy.

Limpy scrambled through the bushes and found himself in a small clearing ringed by trees.

He stared in horror.

At the edge of the clearing stood Goliath, wavy mud stripes gleaming in the sunlight, holding the biggest sharp stick Limpy had ever seen. Lined up in front of Goliath were quite a few other cane toads, including Mum and Dad and Charm. They were also covered in wavy mud stripes and holding sharp sticks.

Limpy felt dizzy with panic.

'Mum,' he croaked. 'What are you all doing?'

Mum and Dad gave Limpy guilty looks, but Charm didn't even look up. She was staring hard at a soft-drink can some distance away on a log. Suddenly she flexed her glands and two little globs of poison pus flew across the clearing and pinged into the can.

Several of the cane toads applauded. Mum and Dad looked proud.

Limpy stared, gobsmacked. He'd always assumed the pollution that had stunted Charm's growth had also stopped her poison glands from developing to full power.

Obviously not.

Stack me, thought Limpy. My little sister's in the army and she's a crack shot.

'I said atten-shun,' yelled Goliath.

The cane toads all stood to attention.

'Charge!' yelled Goliath.

The cane toads charged.

For a sickening heartbeat Limpy thought they were attacking the human picnickers. He hopped forward to fling himself at them. There were too many for him to stop them all, but at least he could grab Mum and Dad and Charm and save them from being stabbed with pie crusts.

Then Limpy realised the cane toads weren't charging at humans, they were charging around a home-made military training course.

Charm was wading through a pit full of those fat bog leeches that explode if you tread on them.

Dad was wriggling on his tummy under low-slung strands of barbed creeper and stinging nettles.

Mum was trying to clamber up a high wall of car hubcaps with the engine grease still on them. She was almost at the top, but was slipping off, waving her arms wildly.

Limpy hurled himself forward and managed to give her something soft to land on.

Him.

'Sorry, love,' panted Mum as she helped him up and pumped air back into his chest. 'I'm not a very good commando.'

'What are you doing here?' wheezed Limpy.

Mum looked at the ground. 'I thought if we defeated the humans in a war,' she said quietly, 'our relatives would stop being squashed on the highway and your room wouldn't get so cluttered.'

Limpy sighed. Mum was always going on about the dead rellies stacked up in his room. He didn't know why. He kept them tidy and dusted.

Dad hobbled over, wincing as he pulled creeper barbs out of his shoulders. 'I just want a little respect,' he said. 'Humans don't have to stop killing us completely, but I just want them to respect us a little more.'

'I want them to stop killing us completely,' said Charm, scowling through the bits of bog leech splattered on her face. 'If they don't, I'll squirt them.'

Limpy stared at his family. He felt weak with shock and the impact of Mum's bottom.

'I thought it was a real battle,' he said. 'I thought you were going to be killed.'

Mum patted Limpy's hand.

'Sorry we didn't tell you about all this,' she said. 'Goliath reckoned you'd chuck a wobbly if you knew we were doing military training, you being a peace lover and all.'

'Actually,' said Dad, 'I think it's Goliath who's chucking the wobbly.'

Goliath was storming towards them, waving his stick in fury.

'This is not good enough,' he roared. 'An army

without training and discipline isn't an army, it's a pathetic rabble.'

'Accept it, love,' said Mum to Goliath. 'That's what we are.'

The other cane toads gathered round, nodding.

Suddenly Limpy didn't feel weak any more. He pulled himself up to his full height, hoping his crook leg wasn't making him tilt over too much, and looked around at the other cane toads.

'I know how you feel,' he said. 'I want to make things better for us too. But starting a war isn't the answer.'

'Why,' demanded Goliath. 'Are you scared we'd lose?'

'Partly,' said Limpy. 'Humans are bigger than us and they have guns and bombs and many other weapons of mass destruction, including pies. But there's a more important reason. If we start trying to hurt and kill humans, that makes us as bad as them.'

The other cane toads thought about this. After a while, quite a few of them croaked their agreement.

Goliath threw his stick away and slumped down into the mud.

'You always spoil my plans,' he complained to Limpy. 'It was the same when I had that great idea about training worms to crawl down our throats and into our tummies while we're asleep.'

Limpy gave one of Goliath's big warts a

sympathetic squeeze. Then he looked around at the other cane toads again. 'There's only one way we can survive,' he said. 'We've got to find a way to live in peace with humans.'

He was just about to say 'and I think we can do it' when the air was filled with a loud mechanical roar.

It was coming from some distance away, but getting closer.

And louder.

Limpy had a horrible thought. The humans must have found out about Goliath's war plans and were attacking first.

'Take cover,' he yelled. 'Watch out for truck tyres and sausage rolls.'

The cane toads scattered. Limpy grabbed Charm. Goliath grabbed Mum and Dad. They all dived into a bog hole at the edge of the clearing.

The engine roar was deafening now and the mud under Limpy's chin was vibrating.

Suddenly, trees on the other side of the clearing started to topple. Something huge was pushing them over. Limpy saw it was a bulldozer driven by one of the human picnickers, who was now wearing a yellow plastic helmet. Two other bulldozers roared into view.

'You mongrels,' yelled Goliath. 'Some of my friends live in those trees. And some of my meals.'

Limpy dragged Goliath back down into the

hole. They all huddled together, deafened by the noise of the bulldozers and the crash of falling timber. Limpy could see Mum and Dad and Charm were glad they weren't out there fighting the bulldozers in a battle.

'Let go of me,' muttered Goliath. 'I'm gunna rip their front bits off and use them to make great big dents in their back bits.'

But Limpy couldn't feel Goliath struggling very hard.

After a long time, the crashing stopped and the roaring got gradually fainter.

Limpy peered out of the hole. The bulldozers had gone. A whole row of trees was flattened.

'Stack me,' gasped Limpy.

It wasn't the fallen trees that took his breath away. It was what lay beyond them in the distance.

Houses.

Streets.

All around the edge of a huge lake.

'Gargling goannas,' said Dad. 'It's a human suburb.'

Limpy stared, stunned. He hadn't even known the lake was there. And he'd had no idea the humans were getting this close.

Goliath stood up and glared at the suburb.

'See,' he growled. 'If we don't do something, the mongrels will keep advancing till they've covered the whole swamp with buildings and roads and concrete. With us buried underneath.'

With a sinking heart and drooping warts, Limpy realised Goliath might be right. The task ahead was going to be harder than he'd thought.

'There's only one way we can save ourselves and the swamp,' said Limpy.

'War,' growled Goliath.

Limpy took a deep breath and started looking around for slugs.

'Friendship,' he said.

Limpy had never been in a human front yard before.

He didn't like it.

They didn't even have a swamp, just a fish pond with a pink concrete bottom. Limpy couldn't see a single mud worm in it, or a single slime leech. No wonder the poor fish looked so stressed. Almost as stressed as Goliath and Charm were looking.

'Goliath,' whispered Limpy. 'Put that stick down. We're on a mission of friendship.'

Goliath scowled. He didn't put the stick down.

Limpy didn't dare yell at him. Not here in the middle of a human suburb in broad daylight. The front yards he and Charm and Goliath were clambering across hid them a bit, but it was still too risky. If a human in a house or a passing car heard croaking and happened to have a high-powered rifle or golf club handy, he and Charm and Goliath would be goners.

Limpy gripped his knotted lizard bladder full of slug sauce and looked nervously up and down the street.

'Remember,' he whispered to the others. 'We're looking for the biggest house.'

'Yeah,' said Goliath. 'So we can blow it up.'

Limpy sighed. 'We're looking for the biggest house because that's where the local human leader must live,' he said. 'The person we're going to give our gifts of friendship to, remember?'

Goliath scowled again.

'Goliath,' said Charm. 'Where's your gift of friendship? The rat rissole?'

'I've got it,' said Goliath indignantly.

Charm looked at him sternly.

'It's in your stomach, isn't it?' she said.

Goliath looked guilty. 'It's safe in there,' he said. 'I put it there so I wouldn't drop it.'

Charm handed Limpy her lizard bladder of maggot moisturiser, clambered up onto Goliath's shoulder and reached into his mouth. She plunged her arm in up to her shoulder, rummaged around, and dragged out a slightly soggy rissole.

'Ow,' said Goliath. 'Your nails are sharp.'

'It's your own fault,' said Limpy, drying the rissole on a leaf. 'You can't give people presents straight out of your stomach.'

'This whole idea's stupid,' said Goliath. 'We shouldn't be giving presents to these mongrels, we should be attacking them, and that's what I'm gunna do.'

Before Limpy could stop him, Goliath had hopped through the fence and was lumbering down the street.

'After him,' said Charm.

They gave chase. Goliath was already a long way ahead. Limpy tried to hop faster, but it was hopeless.

With my crook leg, he thought desperately, and Charm weighed down with presents, we'll never catch him. And even if we do we probably won't be able to calm him down, not even if we use a golf club.

'Goliath,' called Limpy, as loud as he dared. 'Stop. You can't attack a whole suburb on your own.'

'I don't think he's attacking the whole suburb,' panted Charm. 'Just that building.'

Limpy peered into the distance. Up ahead was a building that sprawled the length of a big carpark. It was the biggest building they'd seen yet.

'That must be the human leader's house,' said Limpy.

Goliath was heading for it, waving a sharp stick.

'Come on,' said Limpy. 'We've got to stop him.'

The human leader's house had hundreds of cars parked around it.

'He must be very important,' said Limpy. 'To have so many visitors.'

Plastic bags were blowing around in the carpark. Limpy and Charm hopped into one for disguise and crinkled their way towards the building, weaving and zig-zagging to avoid the cars and other vehicles, which were mostly big wire baskets on wheels.

'These baskets must be so visitors can wheel their gifts over to the human leader's place,' said Limpy. 'Must be big gifts. Makes ours seem a bit small.'

'It's the quality of a gift that counts,' said Charm. 'We could have brought a giant dung beetle but we didn't cause they're all gristle.'

'Good point,' said Limpy.

When they got to the entrance, they both stopped, peering through a split in the plastic bag.

The bag sagged. So did Limpy.

The big glass doors that slid open each time a human approached must be security doors. Even if Limpy could find out the password, he knew he'd never be able to say it.

'Only one thing to do,' he whispered to Charm. 'Get a human to take us in.'

Limpy and Charm clung to each other and tried to make themselves as small as they could.

It wasn't easy for Limpy because he had a big lump in his throat. Pride mostly, and love. How many cane toads had little sisters who would hop into a human's handbag without a croak of

20

complaint, and could do it in the tiny amount of time it took the human to lock her car, drop her keys, pick them up and check her hair in the side mirror?

And that was as well as Charm being a crack shot with her poison pus.

'You're incredible,' Limpy whispered.

'No I'm not,' said Charm. 'I'm just trying to be like you. I always have.'

The feelings inside Limpy were so big he was amazed there was enough room in the handbag for him and the presents and Charm and all the used tissues crumpled up around them.

He gave Charm a grateful hug. Then he listened carefully, trying not to be distracted by the clattering noise of the wire basket wheels underneath him.

There it was.

The hiss of the automatic doors opening.

Limpy grabbed Charm's hand and they struggled up through the damp tissues and peeked out of the handbag.

Stack me, thought Limpy. The human leader's house is full of food.

They were in the biggest room Limpy had ever seen. Shelves loaded with packets and tins stretched away into the distance. Between them were shiny strips of floor as big as highways.

Limpy stared, amazed. Even the newspapers that picnickers sometimes wiped their bottoms on didn't have pictures of this many grocery items.

Charm was staring too.

'Limpy,' she whispered. 'I don't think this is the human leader's house. I think we've come to the wrong place.'

'What do you mean?' asked Limpy.

'I met a weevil once who used to go to places like this for his holidays,' said Charm, eyes wide with concern. 'We're in a supermarket.'

Limpy had a powerful urge to stay in the human's handbag for the rest of his life, or at least until they were out of the supermarket.

As he peeked out, the lights were so bright they hurt his eyes, and the air was colder than swamp mist on a winter morning. He wanted to grab Charm and snuggle back down into the tissues, where he was pretty sure there were interesting morsels to eat.

But he knew they couldn't.

The human was studying some bottles on a shelf. At any moment she could be reaching into her bag for a tissue or a bottle opener.

'Come on,' Limpy whispered to Charm. 'Hop for it.'

They clambered out of the handbag, leaped onto the nearest shelf and hid behind a row of boxes. Limpy stared at the picture on the boxes. A human kid in pyjamas was happily pouring milk onto what looked like a bowl of warts.

Limpy shuddered.

Did humans eat toad warts for breakfast?

He made himself stop thinking about that and follow Charm, who was heading down the narrow space that ran along the back of the shelf.

You're right, Charm, he thought. Concentrate on the job at hand. This is probably the biggest shop in the district. The human leader probably comes here to do his shopping. If we can find him we can give him our gifts of friendship here.

Suddenly Limpy felt more cheerful, even though the cold air was making his warts ache.

Good on you Charm, he thought. You're an inspiration.

Then he remembered the other thing they had to do.

Find Goliath before he started a war.

Along the shelf, Limpy saw that several battles had already taken place.

The first had involved Goliath and a packet of white powder. The human on the front of the packet had several holes in her legs, and Limpy saw immediately that she'd been stabbed with a sharp stick.

'He must be practising before he starts on real humans,' muttered Limpy.

'Oh, Goliath,' sighed Charm. 'Don't do it.'

They followed Goliath's white footsteps and on

another shelf, a very cold one, they found a packet of cheese slices completely ripped open.

Limpy and Charm looked at each other. With Goliath it was hard to know if this was a commando raid or a lunch break.

Then Limpy saw Goliath and gave a croak of alarm.

Goliath was behind another glass door, inside a kind of cupboard or cabinet, surrounded by pizzas. Except, strangely, Goliath wasn't trying to eat the pizzas. He was standing completely still, which Limpy had never seen him do when he was close to even a tiny piece of pizza.

Then Limpy saw something else.

One of Goliath's back legs was raised and a stream of liquid was coming out from behind it.

Limpy felt faint.

'He's peeing on the pizzas,' croaked Limpy. 'And I don't think he's doing it out of friendship.'

Then Limpy noticed something that made him feel puzzled as well as horrified. Something strange about the pee. It wasn't moving. It wasn't splashing on the pizzas. It was just sort of hanging in the air.

Limpy didn't get it.

'Oh, no,' said Charm. 'See how everything in there's got a coating of white on it? I think that's frost. A bird that migrates to our swamp each summer told me there are places so cold that living things go solid and die. It's called freezing. I think that's what Goliath's doing.'

Limpy stared at Goliath.

He certainly looked pretty frosty. And a bit blue.

They had to move fast.

Limpy saw that on the shelf above Goliath were bags of those little round green vegetables that humans sometimes put in rice salads. He couldn't remember what they were called but he saw that a human shopper standing nearby had a bag of the same little frozen green balls in his big wire basket on wheels.

'Stay here,' Limpy said to Charm, and hopped into the basket.

Using both hands and his good foot, Limpy ripped the bag open. The green balls poured out and clattered across the floor.

Limpy ducked behind a carton of milk and held his breath while the human shopper looked at the escaping green balls, frowned, glanced around, then opened the glass door and reached for another bag.

Now, thought Limpy.

He dropped to the floor, lunged into the cabinet, grabbed Goliath and tried to drag him out. Goliath didn't move. Limpy saw the problem. Goliath was frozen to the pizzas with pee. Limpy hauled with all his strength. Suddenly Goliath's frozen pee snapped and Goliath slid out of the cabinet, thudding on top of Limpy.

Goliath's skin was so cold it hurt Limpy's hands. Worse, Goliath's eyeballs weren't moving and his arms and legs didn't seem to be working.

Limpy checked that the shopper, who was hurrying guiltily away from the green balls on the floor, hadn't spotted him and Goliath. He squeezed out from under Goliath and signalled frantically to Charm to come and help.

They rubbed Goliath's frosty warts and massaged his arms and legs.

'Don't die, Goliath,' pleaded Limpy. 'You're a pain in the bum but we love you.'

Goliath's glands gave a faint quiver.

'Keep rubbing,' said Limpy to Charm. 'I just wish we had something warm to wrap him in. A few mouse intestines, something like that.'

'His ankles are starting to thaw,' said Charm.

Suddenly, with a splintering of ice and a lot of groaning, Goliath sat up.

'Are you OK?' asked Charm anxiously.

'My stick,' moaned Goliath. 'Where's my stick?'

'Forget it,' said Limpy. 'We're getting you out of here.'

'We have to defend ourselves,' said Goliath.

At first Limpy didn't understand what Goliath was on about.

Then he heard human voices shouting angrily.

He looked up and nearly fainted. Several human shoppers were advancing towards them, faces twisted with hatred, brandishing big cans and packets and vicious-looking vegetables.

Limpy grabbed the gifts of friendship and turned to face the advancing humans.

Out of the corner of his eye his saw Goliath, shivering with cold and indignation, snatch a cheese stick off a shelf.

'No, Goliath,' begged Limpy. 'Don't.'

It was too late.

'Come on, you wartless wonders,' Goliath yelled at the humans. He waved the cheese stick. 'Do your worst.'

A couple of the humans dropped the groceries they were brandishing and grabbed gardening tools off another shelf. Sharp-looking ones.

Limpy knew the humans' worst would probably involve a lot of stabbing, and then him and Charm and Goliath spending all eternity on a human mantelpiece stuffed with cotton wool or, even worse, dried lentils.

Not if he could help it.

Limpy hopped into the middle of the wide strip of floor, right in front of the humans, and held out the slug sauce and the maggot moisturiser and the rat rissole.

'We come in peace,' he yelled. 'We just want to be friends.'

He knew the humans couldn't understand what he was saying, but he prayed the quality of the gifts would speak for themselves.

Sadly they didn't.

The humans raised their weapons and kept on coming.

Limpy stayed where he was to distract the humans so Charm and Goliath would have one last chance to get away. He closed his eyes and waited to die. While he waited he wished he'd had a chance to say goodbye to his dear sister and cousin. And to Mum and Dad. And to all the dead rellies in his bedroom.

Too late. Limpy felt revolting soft human skin against his own, and then he was lifted high into the air.

He opened his eyes so the human who was about to kill him would know he was a proud fearless cane toad, and also so he could see where to squirt his poison pus.

But the human face looking down at him wasn't twisted with anger and hatred like most human faces. It was peering at him with sympathy.

Limpy saw the face belonged to a teenage girl. She placed him gently into the plastic basket she was holding. Limpy trembled with relief. Charm and Goliath were already in there, both still alive.

'She took my cheese stick,' complained Goliath.

'Shhhh,' said Charm. 'I'm trying to work out what the human's saying.'

The girl was saying something to the other humans. Limpy couldn't understand the words, but he could see, through the lattice of the basket, that the humans had lowered their weapons.

She must be explaining about the presents, thought Limpy. He groped around for the gifts, but Goliath was sitting on the sauce and moisturiser and was eating the rissole again.

Before Limpy could grab the gifts, the basket tilted and Limpy slid into the others. He felt the basket moving at speed. The girl was carrying them through a huge room stacked with cardboard boxes. Then suddenly they were outside and she was carrying them across a carpark full of big trucks.

The girl put the basket down on the ground.

Limpy was about to thank her and offer her some slug sauce, but before he could she lifted him and Charm gently out of the basket and lowered them towards a big muddy tyre rut filled with water.

The water embraced them both and they snuggled down into its depths and Limpy drank some of it gratefully in through his skin.

He looked up at the girl. Against the sky he saw her wobbly outline. As the muddy water moved over Limpy's eyes it played tricks with his vision. One moment the girl's face looked rumpled and warty and friendly, the next it looked smooth and cold and scary.

Limpy felt a jolt of panic. Where was Goliath? Was the girl going to punish him for being threatening with a cheese stick?

No, Limpy saw with relief, she wasn't.

She was carefully placing Goliath in the water next to him and Charm. He heard the slurp of Goliath drinking in water through his skin.

Stack me, thought Limpy. A human has saved our lives.

He looked up through the water again. The girl was moving away, but he got another good look at her face before she disappeared.

It was definitely friendly.

Suddenly Limpy knew this was his big chance. He groped around in the water, grabbed the bladders of sauce and moisturiser, and hopped out into the sunlight.

Charm's anxious voice bubbled up from the water.

'Limpy, where are you going?'

'Don't worry,' called Limpy as he headed after the girl. 'This could be the answer to all our problems.'

At first Limpy thought he'd lost the girl in the huge room full of cardboard boxes. Then he saw her, in a small room to one side with a table in it and some chairs.

She was pouring a drink into a glass and talking to a couple of other humans who were wearing exactly the same clothes as her. Limpy realised they were uniforms. He'd seen humans wearing uniforms on bushwalks. Either the girl worked at the supermarket or she was a bus driver.

Doesn't matter what her job is, thought Limpy excitedly. The important thing is she can teach me how to make friends with humans. Who knows where it might lead? Peace and friendship between humans and cane toads everywhere, for example. Including on picnics.

The other uniformed people left the room, and the girl sat down and sipped her drink.

Now, thought Limpy.

He hopped into the room, holding out the slug sauce and the maggot moisturiser.

Before he could catch the girl's attention, she put her drink down, stood up and went to the other side of the room.

Limpy waited patiently for her to turn round and see him. She was washing her hands at the sink.

Good, thought Limpy. She'll probably need moisturiser after using soap. Goliath does whenever he eats some.

The girl moved away from the sink and opened the door of a white cupboard that was making the same low rumbling noise Dad made when he snored. For a crazy moment Limpy thought the cupboard was full of sleeping cane toads. Then the girl reached in and took out a leg and started eating it.

It was, Limpy saw with relief, a chicken leg, not a cane toad leg.

The white cupboard must be full of sleeping chickens.

The girl was also holding a carrot. She headed back towards the sink. Limpy opened his skin pores and took a deep breath through them so he'd be nice and relaxed when she saw him. As he did, he spotted something that made him clam them up again with panic.

Charm was next to the table leg, waving to him frantically and pointing at something.

Goliath.

He was up on the girl's chair, hands on hips.

Peeing into her drink.

Limpy went weak at the warts. Before he could do anything, the girl turned and headed towards the chair, humming.

Limpy shrank into the shadows under the table.

Goliath dived for the door. Charm followed, frantically signalling for Limpy to come too.

The girl sat down, took another bite of chicken leg, and picked up her drink.

Limpy stared in horror. Then, praying his crook leg wouldn't send him spinning into the sink, he dropped the gifts and hopped onto the arm of the girl's chair and flung himself at the glass just as she was lifting it to her lips.

Limpy smacked into the glass so hard he nearly swallowed his tongue and one of his eyelids.

The glass spun through the air.

So did Limpy.

The glass landed on the floor and smashed.

So did Limpy, except when he wiped the sticky liquid out of his eyes he found he hadn't actually broken anything, he just felt like he had.

He stood up, aching all over.

The girl was on her feet, staring down at him.

Limpy didn't hang around to say g'day. He tottered out the door and crawled through a pile of rubbish after Charm and Goliath.

'Goliath,' he croaked, once they were out of the building and safe in the thick undergrowth at the back of the carpark. 'Why did you do that?'

Goliath glared back towards the supermarket. 'Because you've gone soft,' he growled. 'Wasting time trying to make friends. If we're gunna win this war, we've got to hit those humans where it hurts. Pee in their drinks. Pee in their beds if we have to.'

Limpy sighed. And not just because his cousin was an idiot. He was remembering the girl's angry face as she stared down at him, so furious she hadn't even noticed the bladders of sauce and moisturiser squashed under her shoes.

It was the face of someone who'd never be his friend now, not even if sludge worms could fly.

6

'I'm gunna train whole battalions of cane toads,' said Goliath, eyes shining. 'And we're gunna pee in every dam, reservoir and car radiator we can find.'

'I think we should pick our targets more carefully,' said Charm, squirting pus at a pair of human trousers hanging on a washing line and hitting them right between the legs. 'That way we won't hurt innocent bystanders. What do you reckon, Limpy?'

Limpy didn't say anything. He was too busy trying to get the three of them safely across this human backyard, and the next, until they were out of the human suburb and out of the hot sun and home in the swamp.

'Don't be depressed, Limpy,' said Charm. 'You did your best. It's not your fault your way didn't work.'

'Luckily we've still got my way,' said Goliath. 'Cream the mongrels.'

'Keep hopping,' said Limpy, glancing anxiously

at the house whose flower beds they were hurrying through. He didn't want an angry human spotting them and making Goliath depressed too. With a chainsaw.

Goliath gave a yell.

'Look. Over there. A prisoner of war.'

Limpy looked.

In a cage was a small bird that was even more colourful than one of Mum's butterfly and wasp casseroles. The cage was hanging from one of those complicated revolving metal things which Goliath reckoned were high-tech military helicopters used by humans to kill cane toads. And to dry clothes.

Goliath was wriggling across the lawn towards the cage on his stomach.

Limpy sighed. Only one more backyard to go and they'd be safely out of the suburb. Why did Goliath have to pick now to do a bad commando impersonation?

'We can't just leave the poor thing a prisoner,' said Charm.

'No,' said Limpy wearily. 'You're right.'

He and Charm followed Goliath to the cage.

'G'day,' said the bird when they got there.

'Just act natural,' Goliath hissed at the bird. 'We're gunna get you out of here. Where are the guards?'

The bird stared at him. 'Guards?' it said. Then it chuckled. 'Don't be dopey. I like it here.'

Limpy frowned in surprise.

Goliath nearly fell over. 'Like it?' he croaked.

'I get six meals a day,' said the bird. 'I've got my own mirror. And I get to fly around the living room on Sundays. What do you reckon?'

'He's been brainwashed,' muttered Goliath to Limpy. 'Military intelligence have washed his brain. And rinsed it.'

'Goliath,' said Charm. 'He's a pet.'

Limpy realised she was right. He knew what pets were. He'd seen them on the back shelves of passing cars. Cats and dogs mostly. They'd seemed pretty happy, judging by how often they nodded their heads.

'A pet?' said Goliath, confused. 'Not a prisoner of war? Then why's he chained to a military clothes drying device?'

Limpy looked pleadingly at Charm, hoping she'd do the explaining so they could leave.

'You lot are cane toads, aren't you?' said the bird.

Limpy nodded.

'I'm related to you,' said the bird.

Now it was Limpy's turn to be confused. The bird had feathers and a beak and not one visible wart.

'I say related,' continued the bird. 'What I really mean is, we come from the same place.'

'Where's that?' asked Goliath suspiciously. 'I've never seen you around the swamp.'

'Pet shop in town,' said the bird. 'The one next to the dry cleaner's. But originally my species and your species both came from the Amazon river region in a place called Brazil. Both been there since time began, apparently. A guinea pig in the pet shop told me.'

Limpy's warts prickled with impatience. He'd heard all this before, when the old cane toads had drunk too much cockroach sherry.

'We've got to go,' he hissed at Charm and Goliath.

'Lovely place, the Amazon, by all accounts,' said the bird. 'You know those ads for New Zealand on TV? From what I've heard the Amazon is even better.'

'What's so lovely about it?' said Goliath. 'Have all the humans there been blown up?'

'Don't think so,' said the bird, giving Goliath a strange look.

In the distance a door slammed.

Limpy stiffened. He squinted towards the house. A human was coming down the steps from the deck, carrying a bag of nuts.

'Ah,' said the bird. 'Afternoon tea.'

'Hop for it,' said Limpy to Charm and Goliath.

They both hesitated. Limpy could see they were thinking about letting the human have it with their weapon of choice.

He grabbed them and dragged them towards the flower bed, crook leg trembling with the effort.

Finally they stopped resisting and the three of them dived under some big leaves. When they'd stopped panting, Limpy noticed Charm wasn't looking at him quite as gratefully as she usually did when he rescued her.

'Limpy,' said Charm. 'I know you want to keep me safe, and I appreciate it, but don't you think I'm getting a bit big for you to be bossing me around?'

'Me too,' grumbled Goliath.

Limpy didn't know what to say. Charm hadn't grown at all since she was little. Neither had Goliath's brain.

'No offence, Limpy,' said Charm gently. 'But if I'm going to be bossed around, I prefer someone a bit old and wise to do it. Someone like Aunty Pru.'

'Me too,' said Goliath. 'Except not Aunty Pru cause she uses long words.'

Limpy stared at Charm, thoughts racing.

Of course. That's what we need. Someone older and wiser to give us advice on how to live in peace with humans.

'You're a genius,' said Limpy, hugging Charm.

'What about me?' said Goliath. 'I had the idea about peeing on the pizzas.'

7

They found Aunty Pru on the road leading out of the suburb. She was staring at something small and flat on the tarmac.

'Aunty Pru,' called Limpy from the edge of the road. 'Can we ask you something?'

Aunty Pru looked up, startled. Then her face broke into a big wrinkled smile as she recognised Limpy and Charm and Goliath.

'G'day, young uns,' she said. 'Fire away, I'm all ears.'

Goliath stared at her, looking confused.

'No she's not,' he whispered to Limpy. 'Most of those are warts.'

Limpy ignored Goliath.

'Aunty Pru,' he said. 'What's the best way of living in peace with humans?'

'A way which doesn't involve going into supermarkets,' said Charm.

'It's war, isn't it?' said Goliath.

Aunty Pru frowned thoughtfully. 'Funny you should ask,' she said. 'I've just been thinking about that.'

She stared at the tarmac again.

For a long time.

'When I said she uses long words,' muttered Goliath, 'I really meant long pauses.'

Finally Aunty Pru spoke again. 'The thing about humans,' she said, 'is they're complicated. Some creatures they like, some creatures they don't like. Dogs, for example, they like. And cats.'

'And birds,' said Charm.

'Some birds,' said Aunty Pru. She pointed to the tarmac at her feet. 'This little bird they drove over and squashed. Come and look.'

Charm and Goliath started to hop towards her. Limpy grabbed them. He shook his head to remind them of the rule.

Never go onto a road unless you really have to.

He knew Aunty Pru would be reminding them of the rule if she wasn't having such deep thoughts.

'I don't think I'll ever understand humans,' Aunty Pru was saying as she stared down at the road.

Limpy heard a distant roar. He looked along the road. A truck was coming.

'Aunty Pru,' he said. 'A truck's coming.'

She didn't seem to have heard him or the truck.

'Aunty Pru,' called Charm. 'Truck approaching.'

Aunty Pru still wasn't looking up. She was just

staring at the flat bird, lost in thought.

'Aunty Pru,' yelled Goliath. 'Move your butt.'

Limpy glanced anxiously at the truck. He saw it was a supermarket truck and it was getting close.

'Aunty Pru,' he screamed. So did Charm.

Limpy hopped forward to grab Aunty Pru but it was already too late. The truck was too close. Charm started to move forward and Limpy grabbed her just in time.

The truck thundered past.

When the dust cleared, Limpy couldn't look.

He didn't have to.

'Aunty Pru,' wailed Charm, and collapsed into sobs.

So did Goliath.

Limpy and the others carried Aunty Pru home. They laid her gently down on the big leaves in the kitchen. The whole family gathered round her poor flat body.

Limpy's warts ached with sadness.

He was sad for Charm too. He'd never seen her so upset. He watched her stroke the tyre tracks on Aunty Pru's face and kidneys and saw she was wearing the necklace Aunty Pru had given her, the one woven from spiders' web with dried mouse eyes threaded on it.

'Aunty Pru was so clever and wise,' sobbed Charm. 'How could she have let a human drive over her?'

Mum and Dad came over and stroked Charm's warts.

'If I told Pru once I told her a million times,' said Dad quietly. 'Have as many big philosophical thoughts as you like, I told her, but when you're on the highway don't eat with your eyes closed.'

'Poor old Pru,' said Mum. 'I'll miss her, and that's saying something because I've still got several hundred sisters left.'

Goliath gave a loud sniff. 'We could have saved her,' he mumbled miserably. 'We could have bashed that truck with big sticks and made it swerve off the highway and explode before it reached Aunty Pru.'

Limpy nodded. He didn't agree with the exploding truck stuff, but he agreed with Goliath's basic point.

They could have saved Aunty Pru.

If we'd managed to make friends with humans, thought Limpy, Aunty Pru needn't have died. If the truck driver had been our friend he wouldn't have swerved at the last second and purposely flattened her.

Thinking about it made Limpy's head hurt, so he concentrated on trying to make Charm feel better.

He gave his sister a hug, careful not to squash Aunty Pru's necklace.

'Aunty Pru was very special,' said Limpy. 'She deserves to be laid to rest in a very special place. At the top of the pile.'

'You'll be lucky,' said Mum. 'You'd need a crowbar to get another dead relative into that room of yours.'

'Thanks, Limpy,' said Charm in a trembling voice. 'But if it's OK, I'd like Aunty Pru in my room.'

'Oh, no,' sighed Mum to Dad. 'Now she's starting.'

Charm gazed at Aunty Pru again.

'She taught me so many wonderful things,' said Charm. 'She taught me about the stars and the seasons and nature and everything.'

'And humans,' said Goliath. 'She taught me not to try and eat them.'

'And she taught us something else,' said Limpy. 'She taught us never to give up, even when a problem seems so huge you just want to crawl into the swamp and put your head under the mud.'

'I always want to do that,' said Goliath.

'If Aunty Pru was still alive,' said Limpy, 'she wouldn't want us to stop trying to be friends with humans.'

'Or trying to kill them,' said Goliath.

Limpy realised Charm was staring at him, her eyes gleaming brighter than the mouse eyes on her necklace.

'You're right, Limpy,' said Charm. 'Aunty Pru was the wisest aunty in the whole swamp. In fact I reckon she was the wisest aunty in the whole world, with the possible exception of some of our rellies in the Amazon. They must be very wise if they've survived there since time began.'

Limpy stared back at Charm.

What he'd said in the human flower bed was right.

Charm was a genius.

Here she was, pale with shock and grief, and she'd still managed to give him the idea that was going to save them all.

8

'Excuse me,' said Limpy to the birds pecking in the mud at the far end of the swamp. 'Are you migratory?'

The largest bird stared at Limpy.

'Who wants to know?' it said.

Limpy tried not to look desperate. It wasn't easy. He'd been searching everywhere for the birds Charm had told him about in the supermarket. The ones from a long way away who migrated to the swamp each year. So far he hadn't been able to find a single one.

'Me,' said Limpy. 'I want to know.'

He tried to keep his throat sac tucked neatly under his chin so he'd look polite and well brought up. Mum always reckoned a floppy throat sac looked awful. Worse than flies with their flies undone.

The bird didn't say anything.

Limpy pressed on. 'I'm trying to find someone

who's been to the Amazon,' he said. 'Have you been to the Amazon?'

'Might have,' said the bird.

Limpy looked at the other birds. They were all staring at him expressionlessly too.

'When you fly back to wherever you come from,' said Limpy as slowly and clearly as he could, 'do you go to or near the Amazon?'

'Might do,' said the bird.

Suddenly Limpy couldn't stand it any longer.

'Stack me,' he exploded. 'This is ridiculous. I give up.'

He turned to go. The birds all burst out laughing.

'Don't mind him,' said another bird to Limpy. 'He's just tugging your tail feathers.'

Limpy stared at them, wondering if it was true that birds' brains were smaller than their beaks.

'Sorry,' chuckled the first bird, wiping his eyes with a wing. 'It's my wicked sense of humour. Only thing that gets me through those long boring flights. Yes, we have been to the Amazon. Top place. We always drop in there for lunch when we're passing.'

Limpy felt like doing cartwheels around the swamp. He controlled himself, except for his mucus which wobbled with excitement.

'Are you going near the Amazon any time in the near future?' he asked.

'Might be,' said the bird.

The other birds all tried to stifle their laughter. One of them swiped the first bird round the head.

'Who wants to know?' chuckled the first bird.

Limpy struggled to stay calm. This was too important to lose your temper over and try to eat birds that were much too big to fit into your mouth.

'Come with me,' said Limpy. 'There's something I want to show you.'

Limpy's room wasn't very big and it was a squash fitting all the birds in, but Limpy managed.

The birds kept on with their jokes, right up until they saw the piles of flat dead rellies.

Then they went very quiet.

'These are uncles,' said Limpy, pointing to a stack in the corner. 'And these are aunties, and these are cousins.'

One of the birds had been leaning its wing on the cousin stack. It hopped away, looking embarrassed.

'You poor bloke,' said the bird. 'We have casualties, but nothing like this. This is like a war.'

Limpy was glad Goliath wasn't around to hear this. It was the day each month that Mum and Dad took Goliath to the waterfall to flush his insides out.

'Have you ever seen anything like this in the Amazon?' Limpy asked the birds.

He half-expected them to say 'who wants to know' but they didn't.

'No,' they said quietly. 'We haven't.'

'So humans in the Amazon don't kill cane toads,' said Limpy.

'Don't think so,' said the birds. 'We've never seen any sign of it.'

It was exactly what Limpy was hoping they'd say.

'I need to go to the Amazon really urgently,' he said. 'My ancestors have been living there since time began, and I need to visit them to learn the ancient secret of how to live in peace with humans.' He took a deep breath. 'Any chance of a lift, please?'

The biggest bird's beak fell open.

He stared at Limpy.

'You're asking me,' he said, 'to carry you halfway round the world, across plains and mountains and cities and oceans, risking wing strain and leg rupture and claw cramp, just so a bunch of your family and friends won't get squashed by humans?'

'Yes,' said Limpy.

The bird stared silently at the piles of rellies.

'OK,' said the bird. 'We're leaving first thing tomorrow.'

After Limpy finished thanking the birds, and they left, he started packing for the trip.

His one worry now was how to tell Mum and Dad.

He was pretty sure the journey to the Amazon would be long and dangerous. What if Mum and

Dad got upset and tried to stop him going? Or, even worse, wanted to come themselves? Crossing plains and mountains and cities and oceans was much too risky for a couple their age.

But he had to let them know he was going so they wouldn't think he'd just disappeared or been arrested by an angry supermarket company.

Suddenly he knew what to do. Once he was airborne, and it was too late for anyone to stop him going, he'd get his bird to swoop low over the swamp so he could tell Mum and Dad he'd be away for a while, but not to worry, he'd be fine and so would they with Charm and Goliath to look after them.

He felt better now he'd decided that.

Then Charm hopped into his room and he didn't feel better any more.

'Have you had birds in here?' said Charm.

Limpy could see she'd spotted some feathers on the floor.

'No,' said Limpy. 'They're just left over from an old lunch of Goliath's.'

He felt awful, lying to Charm. His insides felt yukky, like the time he ate the car deodorant block Goliath gave him for his birthday.

Charm's face fell, and Limpy could see she knew he was lying.

He couldn't bear it.

'Yes,' he said quietly. 'I have had birds in here. They're going to take me to the Amazon so I can find out how our rellies there live in peace with humans. I didn't want you to know in case you wanted to come. I don't want you to come because it'll be too dangerous and I don't want anything to happen to you.'

Limpy hoped Charm wouldn't be angry.

She didn't seem to be. She was gazing at Limpy, mouth trembling. She put her arms around him.

'I love you, Limpy,' said Charm. 'And I'm really glad you're my brother.'

'I love you too,' said Limpy.

They hugged each other for a long time.

'There's something I haven't had a chance to tell you,' said Charm. 'You were really brave, the way you saved Goliath from that supermarket freezer. And the way you saved that human girl from that drink. And it wasn't your fault we couldn't save Aunty Pru.'

'Thanks,' whispered Limpy.

I'll miss you, Charm, he thought sadly, trying to stop his glands from trembling too much.

Suddenly he was hoping the journey to the Amazon wouldn't be too long and dangerous.

9

'Goliath,' whispered Limpy. 'Wake up.'

Goliath moaned and tried to wriggle deeper into the mud puddle he was sleeping in. He opened an eye, then closed it.

'No,' he said. 'It's not even dawn yet.'

'We're going to be late,' said Limpy. 'It's taken me ages to find you. Why can't you sleep in your room?'

'It's better out here,' mumbled Goliath. 'If you're lucky, worms crawl into your tummy while you're asleep.' He opened an eye again. 'Late for what?'

'We're going to the Amazon,' said Limpy.

Goliath sat up, eyes open wide.

'The Amazon?' he said. 'Good idea. We can get all the cane toads over there to join our army and crush those mongrel humans forever. And blow up their freezers.'

Limpy sighed.

He'd agonised most of the night about whether

to bring Goliath on the trip. He'd finally decided he had to. It was the only way he could keep an eye on Goliath and stop him starting wars.

Please let it be the right decision, thought Limpy while Goliath had a stretch and checked under his eyelids for breakfast.

The first wart-blush of dawn was creeping into the sky. Limpy grabbed Goliath's hand and led him quickly towards the far end of the swamp.

'How are we getting to the Amazon?' asked Goliath.

'By air,' said Limpy. 'Some birds are taking us.'

'Ripper,' said Goliath. 'I want the fastest one.'

Even as he was saying this, something swooped low over their heads. They both looked up.

'That's not fair,' said Goliath. 'Charm got first pick.'

Limpy stared upwards. He desperately wanted Goliath to be wrong as usual, but the bird turned and swooped low again and Limpy saw with a jolt of panic that Goliath was right.

Gripped in the bird's claws was Charm.

'Sorry, Limpy,' she yelled. 'But I can't let you do it. Brazil's much too far for a bloke with a crook leg. Tell Mum and Dad I'll be away a while, but not to worry, I'll be fine.'

Limpy could barely hear her last words, because the bird was already heading for the blood-red horizon.

'Come on,' Limpy yelled at Goliath as other

birds swooped over their heads. 'We can't let her go on her own.'

Limpy burst through the bushes at the far end of the swamp and almost fainted with relief.

There were two birds left.

'They're still here,' yelled Goliath.

'Don't get your beak in a twist,' said one of the birds, looking up from the mud he was pecking at. 'We're having a late breakfast. Is that a crime?'

'No need to get your wings in a knot,' said the other bird to Limpy. 'Your sister's gone instead. And I personally think she'll do a better job, because in my experience girls are better at quests that involve being polite and asking questions.'

'We need to go too,' said Limpy. 'Right now.'

Before the birds could answer, Mum and Dad burst through the bushes, looking distraught.

'We saw Charm flying away,' said Mum. 'Where's she going?'

Limpy tried to think what to say that wouldn't upset Mum and Dad even more.

'She's going to the Amazon to find the ancient secret of how to deal with humans,' said Goliath. 'But don't worry, we're going too, so it'll be OK. We probably won't all be killed so at least one of us'll make it back.'

Limpy wished Goliath was somewhere else. Like under the mud.

Mum and Dad's faces fell further.

So did Goliath's when he realised what he'd said.

'On second thoughts,' he mumbled, 'perhaps none of us should go.'

The two birds looked at each other, then at Goliath.

'He does look a bit heavy to carry,' said the first bird.

To Limpy's surprise, Mum spoke up.

'No he's not,' said Mum. 'It's mostly wind.'

'Show them, Goliath,' said Dad.

Goliath let out a lot of wind, fast and loud.

'See?' said Mum. 'Get him airborne and he'll help you catch up to our daughter in no time.'

The take-off was fine.

Sort of.

Limpy and Goliath waved to Mum and Dad, and they both waved back. Limpy saw pride on their faces as well as concern.

'Try not to worry,' he called to them.

'That's right,' yelled Goliath. 'We'll be back safely before you can say Aunty Pru.'

Limpy hid his head.

The birds carried them higher, over the human suburb. Limpy looked down at the tiny humans starting their day. They didn't look so scary that size, and Limpy was filled with a happy feeling.

This quest was going to be a success, he was certain.

Then he saw that Goliath was scowling and

doing a pee onto the supermarket far below.

OK, thought Limpy. Almost certain.

Once the birds reached cruising altitude Goliath's warts turned pale and he started to panic.

'Can you fly a bit lower?' he said to his bird. 'It's not that I'm scared of heights or anything. I'm just trying to spot more human targets so we can do more bombing runs.'

Goliath's bird ignored him.

'All right,' wailed Goliath. 'I am scared of heights.'

His bird still ignored him.

Limpy wasn't enjoying the flight either, and he didn't mind heights. He didn't even mind his bird's claws digging painfully into the loose skin at the back of his neck, or the cold air making his warts and eyeballs ache.

What he hated was how, apart from a few clouds, the sky ahead was completely empty. Not a sign of Charm.

Limpy tried not to think of the awful things that could be happening to his little sister. Lightning strikes. Thunderstorms with hail the size of mice. Attacks by eagles or ducks.

He tried to console himself by thinking about Charm's strengths. He knew she could look after herself, he'd seen her do it loads of times. She could disable a killer wombat just with tickling.

But she'd never done it this high up.

'Excuse me,' Limpy said to his bird. 'Any chance of flying a bit faster?'

'Excuse me,' said his bird. 'This is a three-day flight. I'm trying to conserve energy. Any chance of reducing wind-drag by keeping your mouth shut?'

After a lot more flying, Goliath started to enjoy the trip.

'This isn't so bad,' he called across to Limpy. 'I really like the in-flight meal service.'

Limpy had to admit it wasn't so bad. Every time the big wings flapped above his head, a shower of tiny lice and mites tumbled down out of the feathers. All you had to do was stick your tongue out.

That's if you could stomach food in the first place.

Limpy's guts were so knotted he had lice and mites knocking on the inside of his mouth asking to be let out.

'Look,' yelled Goliath. 'Humans.'

Limpy peered down. Goliath was right. They were flying over the outskirts of a city. Limpy could see roads and buildings and those places where humans took their cars for a drink.

'Get your mucus into lumps, everyone,' yelled Goliath. 'We'll bomb the mongrels.'

'Or, alternatively,' said Goliath's bird, 'some of us could use our mucus to block our mouths up so we can have some peace and quiet.'

Limpy didn't join in this discussion. He was too busy staring ahead, excitement surging through him about what he could suddenly see in the distance. Several birds, wheeling in a circle. Birds like the ones he and Goliath were travelling with.

Dangling from the claws of one was a tiny figure.

Limpy couldn't see her face, but he recognised the determined shape of her shoulders and the way her legs were flapping behind her just like they did when Dad spun her round by her poison glands.

'Charm,' screamed Limpy.

He tugged frantically at his bird's ankles.

'We've got to catch up with her,' he yelled.

'Excuse me,' said Limpy's bird. 'I do distance. If you wanted speed you should have waited for a sparrow.'

Suddenly Limpy stopped listening. He almost stopped breathing. He stared helplessly at the awful, horrible, terrible thing that was happening up ahead.

Charm wasn't dangling from her bird's claws any more.

She was falling, tumbling, plummeting towards the ground.

10

'Charm,' yelled Limpy.

'He's dropped her,' screamed Goliath.

'Excuse me,' said Goliath's bird. 'We don't drop passengers. If she's finishing her flight here it's because she wants to.'

Limpy had never heard such rubbish. This wasn't the Amazon. They hadn't travelled nearly far enough. And anyway, who would want to end a journey falling from this height onto a big area of concrete?

'No,' croaked Limpy.

He couldn't take his eyes off his dear plummeting sister. He didn't want to look, but he couldn't stop himself.

Poor thing. She'd come all this way only to end up as flat and dead as if she'd stayed at home.

Unless . . .

'She's gunna hit that bus,' screamed Goliath.

Limpy's bird was swooping low now and Limpy

could see Charm tumbling towards a big tourist bus parked next to a building. But she didn't hit the bus, she disappeared behind it. For a brief moment Limpy couldn't see her. Then the swoop carried him up again and there she was, on the other side of the bus, lying face-down on top of a big pile of human tourist bags.

Arms and legs stuck out straight.

Not moving.

'Drop us,' yelled Limpy.

'Excuse me,' said his bird. 'You heard what my colleague said. We don't drop.'

'That's an airport down there,' said Goliath's bird. 'Airports are made of concrete. You're made of squishy stuff. You do the sums.'

'I don't care,' said Limpy. 'Drop us.'

He saw it was too late. They were already flying past the airport. He twisted round, desperately trying to see a landmark he could use to find his way back to Charm.

That tower with the windows in the top.

'My cousin said drop us,' yelled Goliath, 'and he meant it.'

'Read my beak,' said Limpy's bird. 'We don't drop.'

'If you don't drop us now,' roared Goliath, 'I'm gunna bite through your ankles.'

'For you two,' said Goliath's bird, 'we'll make an exception.'

* * *

The fall was scary.

Limpy took his mind off it by thinking about Charm. Her sweet face. Her kind nature. They way she could scare off wild bush pigs just by giving them maths problems.

The landing was fairly soft. And very smelly.

'Yuk,' said Goliath, spitting and rubbing his eyes. 'Human poo.'

It was. Once Limpy's head stopped spinning, he looked around in amazement. He'd never seen so much in one place. Swamp-loads of it.

'It's a sewage farm,' said a blowfly sunbathing nearby.

'A farm?' said Goliath, amazed. 'You mean humans don't produce enough of this stuff themselves so they grow more?'

Limpy remembered they were in the middle of a family tragedy.

'Goliath,' he said, trembling. 'We have to find Charm.'

Goliath's face fell.

'I know,' he said sadly. 'I was trying not to think about it.' He smacked a big fist into a warty palm. 'I hate those mongrel humans with their vicious pies and poo farms. When I get my army together I'm gunna flatten those mongrels for killing Charm.'

Limpy sighed.

'We don't have time for this now,' he said. 'Charm might not be dead. She might just be hurt.'

'Yeah, well even if she is just hurt,' said Goliath, 'it's still those mongrels' fault. They're the ones whose truck squashed your leg when you were little. Charm only did this trip cause of your crook leg.'

Limpy stared at Goliath.

He was right.

Dad always reckoned it was no use crying over squashed legs, and Limpy usually agreed, but suddenly he didn't any more.

Suddenly anger stabbed through him and made his warts burn.

If he had two good legs, Charm wouldn't have risked her life like this.

It was the humans' fault.

Limpy closed his eyes and imagined a whole suburb of humans guzzling drinks while Goliath stood nearby, his bladder completely drained.

Then Limpy remembered Charm. He thought about her lying on the bags, in pain, waiting for him and Goliath to come.

He opened his eyes, blinked away the angry feelings, and grabbed Goliath.

'Come on,' he said.

The airport tarmac was very busy.

Birds and insects from all over Australia and many other parts of the world were landing and taking off continuously.

The individual in charge seemed to be a

weary-looking cockroach. He was waving air traffic in and out with what looked at first to Limpy like a couple of table tennis bats. When Limpy got closer he saw they were actually moth wings. The moth was standing at the edge of the tarmac looking annoyed.

'Excuse me,' said Limpy to the cockroach. 'Have you got a moment?'

'Make it snappy,' said the cockroach. 'I've got butterflies from Africa on approach and stink beetles in a holding pattern.'

'We're looking for my sister,' said Limpy. 'She was on a pile of luggage next to a bus, but the bus and the luggage have gone.'

'This is an airport,' said the cockroach. 'Buses and luggage don't hang around.' He paused in the middle of landing a pelican and peered at Limpy. 'There was one of your lot here just now. Cute kid. On her way to the Amazon.'

'That's her,' yelled Limpy.

'Excuse me,' said Goliath to the cockroach. 'That pelican just crashed.'

The cockroach ignored Goliath. 'You've missed her,' he said to Limpy. 'She took off ten minutes ago.'

'So she's OK?' said Limpy, giddy with relief.

'Bit knocked about,' said the cockroach. 'But not too bad. Nowhere near as bruised as that pelican, for example.'

'Which bird did she leave with?' said Limpy.

'And where can we find two more?'

'It wasn't a bird,' said the cockroach. 'It was a plane.'

Limpy knew what planes were. Those huge shiny metal things over in the human part of the airport. Like slugs, but with wings. And much faster.

'There isn't a direct plane flight from here to the Amazon,' said the cockroach, waving in the African butterflies. 'Your sister's gone via Los Angeles. Next plane to LA is that one over there leaving in about four hours.'

Limpy stared across at the huge plane. 'What's the best way to get on it?' he wondered out loud.

'I'll get a sharp stick and bash a hole in the side,' said Goliath.

'Lots of ways in,' said the cockroach, waving the stink beetles out of the butterflies' airspace. 'Once you're on board, find yourself a comfortable pozzie before the human passengers get on. Stay away from those big things under the wings, they'll suck your eyeballs out. I prefer the overhead luggage compartments myself.'

11

The overhead luggage compartments were nice and roomy with attractive decor, but Limpy was worried they were too dangerous. The plane would soon be filling up with passengers and Limpy had noticed how human hand-luggage was mostly heavy bottles.

'We could hide in these paper bags,' suggested Goliath.

Limpy looked at the paper bags Goliath had pulled out of the seat pockets. He wasn't sure what they were for, so he shook his head.

'You never like my ideas,' complained Goliath.

'I'm not saying it's a bad idea,' said Limpy. 'It's just that those bags remind me of the ones moths use when they hit air turbulence. You know, sick bags.'

'So what?' said Goliath, 'There'd be room for us in there as well.'

Limpy decided not to get into an argument

about it. There wasn't time. The human passengers would be getting on the plane very soon and Limpy knew he and Goliath wouldn't pass as flight attendants, not even if they did their nicest smiles.

'Look,' said Limpy. 'Here's a good hiding place. Under the seat next to this rolled-up plastic thing.'

It was a good hiding place.

The passengers got on and Limpy and Goliath weren't discovered, not even when Goliath gave a loud whimper during take-off.

Limpy nearly gave a whimper himself when he saw how close the nearest human feet were. He was glad he and Goliath had been able to wedge themselves under the strap holding the rolled-up plastic thing to the underside of the seat.

'Ow,' said Goliath. 'My ears just popped.'

'Don't worry,' said Limpy. 'I think it's normal.'

'A couple of my warts have popped too,' said Goliath.

Limpy wasn't sure if that was quite so normal.

'I hate planes,' grumbled Goliath. 'They're cold and noisy and cramped and this rolled-up plastic tastes yukky.'

Limpy sighed.

'What about poor Charm,' he said. 'She had to do this all by herself.'

He tried not to think about Charm hiding in an overhead luggage compartment in her plane, or in a paper bag, or even worse, in one of the engines.

Instead he reminded himself what a sensible sister she was. She wouldn't do anything stupid, not on such an important quest.

The thought made Limpy feel better. Goliath seemed to be calming down too.

'You're right,' said Goliath quietly. 'I'm being selfish. This is a good hiding place. When does the in-flight meal service start?'

'Limpy,' said Goliath. 'I don't think this is such a good hiding place after all.'

Limpy was trying to have a doze to take his mind off Charm. In his imagination he was in the Amazon, learning the secrets of a peaceful life from happy peaceful cane toads and happy peaceful humans and a very happy and peaceful tree fungus.

'Limpy,' repeated Goliath, more urgently.

Limpy sighed but didn't open his eyes.

Why can't Goliath ever stop complaining, he thought wearily. OK, it is a bit cramped under this seat, and this strap cuts into your warts something chronic, but it's not all bad. There's a feast of crumbs and food scraps under here and Goliath really enjoyed that lump of old bubble gum he found.

'Limpy,' said Goliath, his voice wobbling. 'Did you hear me?'

Limpy felt himself getting cross. He took a deep breath through his skin pores and reminded himself that poor Goliath had a good reason for being a whinger. His parents had split when he was very young. A truck had run over them and they'd each ended up completely split in half.

'Limpy,' said Goliath, sounding really upset now.

Limpy opened his eyes to ask Goliath to try and forget he was an abandoned child and to be patient for the sake of cane toads everywhere.

The croak froze in his throat as he saw what was peeking at him and Goliath under the edge of the seat.

Two upside-down human faces.

It could have been worse, thought Limpy.

The humans could have been angry violent adults.

These two nice little kids are much better, decided Limpy. Specially as they just want to play with us instead of bashing us with heavy hand-luggage.

Limpy tried to stay as quiet as he could. He didn't want to wake the kids' parents, who were dozing in their seats with the cabin lights off. But the game the kids were playing made that a bit difficult.

'Ooh,' giggled Limpy. 'That tickles.'

'I know what you mean,' muttered Goliath.

Limpy had never worn dolls clothes before. They felt strange, but it was partly because the army outfit the boy was putting on him was a bit tight around the tummy.

The boy put an army helmet onto Limpy's head. It was a bit tight too, but Limpy didn't mind because the boy was grinning happily.

So this is what it feels like to be friends with a human, thought Limpy, grinning happily too.

While the boy struggled to clip an army belt round Limpy's middle, Limpy wondered if this was the ancient secret his rellies in the Amazon had discovered. That humans don't hurt you as long as you let them dress you up.

Later on, the kids fell asleep.

Limpy turned round slowly on the boy's knee, careful not to wake him.

'Goliath,' whispered Limpy. 'Are you OK?'

'No,' said Goliath, wriggling uncomfortably on the girl's lap. 'My dress is too small.'

'I think it looks nice,' said Limpy.

'These earrings are stabbing my ears,' said Goliath.

'That's a shame,' said Limpy. 'They match your eyes.'

'And these shoes are killing my feet,' said Goliath. 'Every time I try and kick them off, I stab myself in the ankles with the high heels.'

Limpy sighed.

Goliath just didn't understand how important it was to the future well-being of cane toads everywhere to be a good pet.

'This is good,' whispered Limpy to Goliath. 'If humans start adopting cane toads as pets, our problems are over.'

'No they're not,' grumbled Goliath. 'This lipstick tastes yuk.'

Limpy had to admit he didn't feel completely good either, but he was pretty sure he would once his new owner worked out his tummy size.

Then Goliath noticed his little girl was asleep.

'I'm out of here,' he muttered.

Before Limpy could stop him, Goliath hopped onto the back of the seat and swung himself across the ceiling of the plane, hanging by his arms.

Limpy went after him, clinging desperately onto reading lights and air-flow nozzles. Luckily most of the passengers were still asleep, and those that were awake were watching a movie on the screen at the front of the cabin.

Limpy prayed none of them would cop a high-heel shoe in the head.

'Goliath,' whispered Limpy. 'Come back. If you start a fight now, it'll delay the next meal.'

Goliath obviously hadn't thought of this, because he stopped so suddenly his wig fell off.

Unfortunately he stopped right in front of the movie projector box. His shadow loomed onto the screen. Limpy got to him as fast as possible and pulled him away.

By then, the passengers watching the movie were on the edges of their seats, thrilled by the sudden brief appearance in a teen love scene of the sinister shadow of a large toad-like monster.

Limpy felt like his brains were going to plop out through his ears.

Relax, he told himself. It's natural to feel like this when you're being carried upside down by one leg, specially in a strange airport.

Limpy hoped the little boy didn't suddenly get over-tired after the long flight and drop him.

He glanced over at Goliath, who was upside down too, clasped by the little girl to her chest.

Goliath didn't look too good.

His dress was bunched up round his neck and his shoes were on back to front. Limpy wasn't sure if he was scowling or just trying to take his earrings off with his mouth.

Hope he doesn't pop a brain-wart, thought Limpy anxiously. If he starts spraying poison pus around here, we're done for.

The kids' parents were standing at a counter showing a couple of small books to a human official. Limpy didn't want to think what the official would do with his gun if Goliath started shooting off at the glands.

Luckily Goliath looked too weary for that.

Then the little girl grabbed Goliath's hand and tried to jam his fingers up his nostrils.

'Baby pick nose,' she said.

Limpy didn't understand what she was saying, and he could see Goliath didn't either, but he hoped it was 'try and stay loose and floppy like your cousin Limpy so the official thinks you're just a stuffed toy or novelty pencil case.'

Whatever the little girl said, it must have worked because when she gave up trying to fit Goliath's big fingers into his nose, Goliath didn't make a fuss. He just looked a bit disappointed and the official waved them all through.

Suddenly they were in the biggest room Limpy had ever seen. It was even bigger than the supermarket, freezer included. Luggage was rumbling round on long flat giant snakes and humans were bumping into each other with big trolleys on wheels.

The kids' father went over towards a luggage snake and their mother bent down and wiped the girl's face with a tissue.

Then she saw Goliath.

'Lucy,' she yelled. 'Where did you get that ghastly thing? Put it down. It's dangerous. Don't touch it.'

Limpy hoped she was saying 'what delightful pets you've both found, we must tell all our friends so they can get their own.'

But when the woman snatched Goliath from the little girl and flung him onto the floor, Limpy knew she probably hadn't said that.

The little girl burst into tears.

The little boy did too, and dropped Limpy.

The woman tried to run Limpy over with a trolley.

Limpy didn't let the army uniform slow him down, or the blow to the head he got from the floor, or his hopes of being a human pet.

He dodged the trolley and grabbed Goliath, who was looking pretty dazed too. Together they hopped around trailers and bags and human feet until Limpy saw a soft-drink machine and dragged Goliath under it.

'I'm never doing dress-ups again,' said Goliath. 'Except for dressing up in mucus to attract slime slugs.'

Limpy felt the same way. As he struggled out of the combat pants he vowed never to wear any sort of pet uniform again. For a start they were too tight and too hard to get off.

Not as tight as high-heel shoes, though. Goliath was having to eat those off.

'Hurry up,' said Limpy. 'So we can find Charm and catch the next plane to the Amazon together.'

Limpy peered out from under the soft-drink machine.

A lot of the humans had gone, including the little kids and their parents, but there were still plenty milling around.

Limpy's insides sank.

'How are we going to find Charm in this huge airport?' he said.

'Easy,' said Goliath, swallowing part of a shoe. 'We'll round up all the humans and put them in a prisoner of war camp, and everyone who's left will either be an insect or an animal or Charm.'

Limpy sighed. Sometimes he wished Goliath's ideas weren't quite so daring. Or quite so stupid.

'I know,' said Limpy. 'We'll find the part of the airport the planes to the Amazon leave from. That's where we'll find Charm.'

A horrible thought hit him.

In an airport this size, planes to the Amazon might leave from different parts. They might go to the wrong part and miss her.

Then Limpy saw something that gave him a fairly daring idea himself.

At a counter nearby, a human was speaking with her mouth close to what looked like a swamp reed stem with a seed pod on top. Her voice was booming out across the arrivals hall.

'Charm would be able to hear that,' said Limpy. 'Even if she's up the other end of the airport.'

Goliath looked embarrassed and patted his stomach.

'I'm sorry, that was a bit loud,' he said. 'Shoes give me wind.'

* * *

75

Limpy and Goliath had to wait quite a long time in the waste bin under the counter.

'Mmmm,' said Goliath. 'This sandwich is deliciously juicy.'

'It's a printer cartridge,' said a passing ant.

Finally the human at the counter was called away, and Limpy seized his chance. He hopped up onto the counter, dragged a box of luggage labels over to the swamp reed stem, hopped onto the box and spoke into the seed pod in his clearest voice.

'Attention, Charm,' he said. 'This is Limpy and Goliath. Don't get on the Amazon plane yet. We're coming with you. Meet us at the . . .'

Where would be a good place to meet?

'Rental car counters,' said Goliath.

Good idea, thought Limpy. He knew what rental cars were. Most of the cars that tried to drive through the bush to remote picnic spots and got bogged in mud holes were rental cars.

'Charm, meet us at the rental car counters,' said Limpy into the seed pod.

He looked around the arrivals hall. As he'd hoped, none of the humans were paying any attention. To them his announcement had probably sounded like an electrical fault. But every other creature in the place was staring, curious and interested.

Good, thought Limpy. Now Charm will turn up in no time.

Charm didn't turn up.

Not even after a lot of time.

Limpy and Goliath searched the whole airport terminal, asking all the insects and rodents and sniffer dogs if they'd seen her.

None of them had.

'I don't trust those sniffer dogs,' muttered Goliath, glaring at the beagles. 'One of them sniffed my bottom. I reckon they've captured Charm and handed her over to their human masters as a war spy.'

Limpy didn't think that was very likely.

They questioned some headlice on the back of a seat in a deserted departure lounge. The headlice hadn't seen Charm, but they told Limpy not to give up, there were three other terminal buildings she could be in.

Limpy sagged with despair.

'This place is too big,' he said to Goliath. 'We'll

never find her.'

'That's if she's here at all,' said Goliath. 'She could be in a child's dolls house over the other side of the city for all we know. Being forced to try on shoes.'

Limpy and Goliath dragged their weary bodies out of the departure lounge in the direction of the next terminal. As they crossed a dusty expanse of tiled floor, Limpy felt dizzy with tiredness. He stopped for a moment to catch his breath.

'Stack me,' said Goliath, pointing to the floor. 'That's Charm.'

Limpy looked down.

And nearly fainted.

He was standing on Charm's head.

Traced in the dust was the outline of Charm's face, bigger than in real life and perfect in every detail. Even her warts were in the right place. Her eyes were as warm and loving as the real things.

'Careful,' said an indignant voice. 'Don't tread on her.'

Limpy, head spinning even more now, staggered off the picture.

A dust mite was glaring at them, claws on hips.

'Did you draw that?' stammered Limpy.

'Yes,' said the dust mite. 'And I don't care who knows it. Fate only brought us together for a few precious minutes, but she won my heart forever. I'd give anything to see her gorgeous face again, but I know I won't, so my love will have to live on in art.'

'Mental,' whispered Goliath in Limpy's ear. 'It's the dust.'

Limpy barely heard him. He was so excited he could hardly speak.

'You've seen my sister?' he croaked.

The dust mite looked startled.

'Sister?' he said, backing away. 'I didn't know she was anyone's sister. Not that anything happened. No kissing or anything. I was just doing a bit of street art. I specialise in old masters, but with more dust. This vision hopped over and asked me how to get to the Amazon. At first I thought she meant that internet bookshop, but she explained she was trying to get to the real Amazon.'

Limpy would have grabbed the dust mite if he'd been able to pick it up. He stepped closer, looming over the terrified artist.

'Did you help her?' he said. 'Has she gone to the Amazon?'

The dust mite nodded.

'We found a weevil who'd spent a lot of time in the air traffic controllers' lunch room. He told her about a flight she'd be able to catch if she hurried.'

Disappointment swept over Limpy like the sour water humans sometimes threw out of their eskies.

'When did she leave?' he said.

'Quite a while ago,' said the dust mite. 'I did her portrait after she left and I can only move one grain of dust at a time.'

'Shall I eat him?' said Goliath.

Limpy shook his head. He had a rule never to eat anyone who felt the same way about Charm as he did, no matter how much he wanted to. Plus he needed travel details.

'This flight Charm caught,' he said. 'When does the next one leave?'

'Not till tomorrow,' said the dust mite. 'And not from this airport. It's a flight that leaves once a day from a private airfield way over in that direction.'

Limpy felt despair rising again.

'It's OK,' said the dust mite. 'You've got all night to get there. I'll draw you a map.'

He started moving grains of dust into the shape of a street. Then he stopped and looked pleadingly up at Limpy.

'When you see her,' he said, 'could you tell her that Myron sends his love.'

Limpy and Goliath took a long time to find their way out of the airport, mostly because Goliath stopped at every food-vending machine to see if he could get his tongue down the coin slot.

Once they were outside and hopping along the dark streets, Goliath announced he wanted to do commando raids on human houses.

'Nothing large scale,' he said. 'Just toilet-splashing and car-scratching.'

Stack me, thought Limpy. At this rate we're never going to get to that airfield.

He said no a lot of times and in a very stern way.

Then, a few streets further on, Goliath hopped away briefly and came back with a tummy ache.

'What did you eat?' Limpy asked anxiously as Goliath lay in the gutter groaning and holding his tummy.

'Just some local food,' said Goliath. 'A snake. At least I think it was a snake.'

Limpy was about to ask him what he meant when a large figure loomed over them. It was an angry poodle.

The poodle pushed Goliath's mouth open, reached down his throat and dragged out a long length of metal chain.

'Don't you be takin' a person's doggy lead, dude,' said the poodle, glaring at Goliath and Limpy.

'Sorry,' said Limpy, as the poodle stamped away in a huff.

'It was shiny like a snake,' protested Goliath.

By the time they finally found the airfield, Goliath was complaining his feet were sore. He hopped through the fence and onto the first plane he saw.

'Goliath,' said Limpy wearily, climbing into a wheel bay and wriggling into the fuselage. 'This is a cropduster.'

Limpy knew about cropdusters. A grasshopper had described once how a cropduster had killed eight million of his family and given his grand-father a skin rash.

'No it's not,' Goliath said.

Limpy pointed to the big tanks of spray inside the cropduster. Goliath looked doubtful and was only convinced when he'd drunk some and his tongue had turned blue.

'Come on,' said Limpy, even more wearily. 'It's getting light outside. Let's find a local who can show us the right plane.'

Limpy jolted awake as the small plane struggled up into the smoggy Los Angeles sky. He breathed a sigh of relief through all his skin pores and several of his warts.

He and Goliath were finally on their way to the Amazon.

'Well done, Goliath,' said Limpy. 'I'm proud of you.'

'Get nicked,' said Goliath. 'My tummy hurts, and my feet, and my tongue.'

Limpy peered into Goliath's mouth. He was relieved to see that Goliath's tongue was almost back to normal.

'Try to relax and enjoy the flight,' said Limpy.

'This plane isn't as good as the one we came over on,' grumbled Goliath. 'There's no movie, or meal service, or seats.'

Limpy had to admit he was right. This plane wasn't much bigger than the cropduster. It was just a hollow metal tube full of empty wooden cages.

'I reckon these cages are to put the passengers in,' said Goliath loudly. 'When they discover there's no meal service and try to throw themselves out the window.'

'Not so loud,' said Limpy. 'There aren't meant to be any passengers. We're stowaways, remember?'

Limpy glanced anxiously through the cages at the pilot, hoping he hadn't heard Goliath's noise.

He didn't seem to have. Limpy could see he was

wearing headphones, and from the way his head was moving rhythmically backwards and forwards, Limpy guessed he was either listening to music or to an air traffic controller he agreed with very much.

Goliath was sifting through the dust on the floor of the plane.

'There's got to be something to eat on this dumb crate,' he said. He peered doubtfully at something in his hand. 'Oh well, this is better than nothing.' He popped it onto his tongue.

Limpy caught a glimpse of it just before Goliath's tongue disappeared into his mouth. He leapt at his startled cousin, pulled his lips apart and dragged his tongue back out.

'Sorry,' said Limpy, warts tingling with excitement. 'But I think I recognise this.'

He plucked the morsel from Goliath's tongue, wiped off the mucus and studied it more closely.

Yes.

It was a dried mouse eye, just like the ones on the necklace Aunty Pru had given Charm.

'This must have fallen off Charm's necklace,' said Limpy. 'She must have been on this plane yesterday. Which means we're on the right track.'

Goliath stared at the mouse eye.

'Poor Charm,' he said. 'Hope the little tyke's OK.'

'So do I,' said Limpy, moved by Goliath's concern.

Goliath took the mouse eye and put it back in his mouth.

'Better keep our strength up,' he said. 'In case she's not.'

Limpy was dozing when he felt Goliath shaking him.

'We're going down,' croaked his cousin.

For a moment Limpy thought Goliath meant the pilot had banged his head on the dashboard during a lively dance number and the plane was crashing.

Then he realised they were coming in for landing.

'There aren't any seat belts,' said Goliath. 'This airline's a joke.'

Limpy dragged a toolbox over to the window, staggering as the plane tilted its nose down even further. He hopped up and peered out.

It was an incredible sight.

Millions of tree tops were jammed together tighter than warts on a warthog. An ocean of thick foliage lay in every direction for as far as Limpy could see, and he could see a long way even though the window was pretty dirty.

'Stack me,' said Limpy. 'This Amazon's a big place.'

He felt the plane starting to level out, so he hopped off the toolbox and huddled down with Goliath, assuming the brace position for landing.

Limpy wasn't sure exactly what the brace position was. A dragonfly had started to explain it once, but Goliath had eaten him before he'd finished. Limpy hoped that clinging onto Goliath and wishing Mum and Dad were here was roughly right.

After a lot of thumps and jolts, the plane rolled to a stop.

Limpy and Goliath stayed huddled out of sight while the pilot flung open the rear door of the plane and dragged out some of the cages.

Must be an urgent delivery, thought Limpy. Must be a lot of people around here with unruly pets.

After a while, when the pilot didn't come back, Limpy peered out of the doorway. He saw the pilot further down the dry grass runway, with a couple of other humans, blowing smoke out of his mouth.

'Come on,' said Limpy to Goliath.

They hopped out of the plane and headed across the runway towards the forest. As they got closer to the dense wall of tangled vegetation, anxious thoughts crash-landed inside Limpy's head.

This place was bigger than a million swamps.

How were they going to find Charm in such a vast area?

Limpy told himself to calm down.

Now she's here, he reminded himself, she'll be fine. This is the ancient home of all cane toads.

The place where our relatives have lived peacefully since the dawn of time.

At this very moment, the local rellies were probably making a big fuss of Charm. As she showed them how to make slug and spider stew the Australian way.

Limpy noticed how almost every tree in the forest he and Goliath were entering had a big creeper wound around it. Tightly, like they were the best of mates. And each creeper had a smaller vine clinging to it in a very affectionate way.

'Stack me,' thought Limpy happily. 'The Amazon rainforest must be the friendliest place on earth.'

Limpy liked the Amazon rainforest even more once he was inside it.

For a start there was no wart-damaging harsh sunlight. Limpy peered up through the green gloom at the tree tops far above. Tiny pricks of sunlight winked through here and there, but not enough to turn warts into breakfast cereal.

Plus it was wonderfully damp. The air was so moist Limpy felt like he was having a drink each time he breathed it in through his skin.

But what Limpy liked most was the smell. Rotting vegetation, his favourite. There was so much fragrant decaying compost under Limpy's feet that when he hopped, he bounced.

I love this place, he thought happily.

'This place is too noisy,' complained Goliath. 'I can't even hear myself complain.'

Limpy grinned.

Goliath was right. The forest was ringing with

countless voices, all shouting at each other. Screeching voices, grunting voices, howling voices, clicking voices, whistling voices, pinging voices, singing voices, gurgling voices and so many more Limpy couldn't make out what a single one was saying.

'Everyone's just relaxed and having fun,' he said.

'I'm not,' said Goliath gloomily. 'I shouldn't even be here. I should be at home with my troops, planning war strategy.'

Limpy sighed.

The sooner we find Charm and our Amazon rellies, he thought, and learn the ancient secret of living in peace and hopefully also the ancient secret of cheering up, the better.

A dazzlingly colourful fly buzzed past Limpy's nose and landed on a strip of orange jelly at Limpy's feet.

'Excuse me,' said Limpy to the fly. 'We've just arrived from Australia and we're looking for my sister. Have you seen anyone who looks a bit like me only prettier?'

The fly ignored him.

'Hey, buster,' said Goliath. 'My cousin's talking to you.'

The fly gave them both a stressed look.

'Go away,' said the fly. 'I'm not a tourist information service. If I don't lay these eggs quick smart, they won't hatch out into maggots and eat this worm from the inside before the rainy season.'

'That's right,' said the orange jelly, who Limpy could now see was a giant worm. 'You holiday-makers just don't get it, do you? We're working here.'

'Sorry,' said Limpy.

Goliath was watching the fly, wide-eyed.

'That's a great secret weapon,' he said. 'Laying eggs under your enemy's skin. Could you teach me how to do that?'

Limpy could see that the fly and the worm were both about to tell Goliath to take a hike, but neither got to because there was a slither and a hiss and they both disappeared into the gaping mouth of a snake.

Limpy hopped back in alarm. Then he realised the snake probably wasn't going to try and fit any more into its mouth, not unless it wanted to risk stretch marks, and seeing Goliath's stretch marks would probably put it off that.

'Excuse me,' said Limpy to the snake. 'Can you help me? I'm looking for my sister and our rellies.'

The snake rolled its eyes and Limpy thought it was saying it couldn't talk because its mouth was full.

In fact, Limpy saw a moment later, it was saying it couldn't talk because a giant spider had just injected a fatal dose of venom into its neck.

Limpy gasped.

He'd never seen a spider bigger than him before.

'Stack me,' said Goliath, sounding scared and impressed at the same time.

Limpy grabbed Goliath and dragged him behind a tree, just as another giant, a wasp this time, plunged its sting into the spider's body.

Limpy felt faint.

The wasp was as big as a human tail light.

The spider stopped sucking the juice out of the snake and rubbed its back legs along the side of its body. A cloud of tiny hairs floated up and covered the wasp, who immediately swelled up and dropped dead.

'Cop that,' muttered the spider, and then dropped dead itself.

Behind the tree, Limpy stared in horror. He glanced at Goliath to see if Goliath was having an anxiety attack. Goliath was staring at the spider in admiration.

'That commando thing with the hairs,' said Goliath. 'I wish I could do that. I wonder if wart flakes would work as well.'

Limpy couldn't speak.

This was a nightmare.

And Charm was somewhere out there, in the middle of it all.

Limpy wasn't sure whether to try and yell her name or not. If the cane toad rellies had her in a safe hiding place and she heard Limpy calling her, she might come out to find him and be killed by some horrible monster.

Like this one arriving now, for example.

Limpy clung on to Goliath and watched as a

huge gangling insect creaked its way over to the dead spider and wasp. Rubbing its long spiky front legs together with relish, the insect grabbed the spider and the wasp and stuffed them into its mouth, ignoring a scorpion who was trying to stab it in the back.

'Wow,' said Goliath. 'Check the armour-plating on that bloke.'

A very big blue and green lizard appeared and bit the insect's head off. The dying insect's twitching legs tried to rip the lizard's scales off, but failed.

'Double wow,' said Goliath. 'Check the armour-plating on that even bigger bloke.'

While the lizard dozed in a thin shaft of sunlight, picking its teeth with the back end of the scorpion, Limpy stayed hidden and tried to get his breath back.

He and Goliath had barely been in the Amazon long enough to say 'peace and friendship,' and already they'd seen creatures ripping each other, crushing each other and inserting maggots into each other.

I hope we can find Charm and the rellies soon, thought Limpy. If Goliath starts trying to eat any of the locals here, we're history.

'There's some very impressive military hardware around here,' said Goliath. 'Very impressive. This tree sap's pretty good too.'

Limpy saw Goliath was chewing lumps of

rubbery sap from the tree next to the one they were hiding behind.

'Tastes like radial tyres,' said Goliath, putting another big lump into his mouth.

Limpy shook his head when Goliath offered him some, partly because his stomach was sick with worry, and partly because of what the lizard was doing.

The lizard was opening one eye and saying 'oh poop, a jaguar.'

A massive yellow cat with black smudges was slinking towards the lizard. It was many times bigger than any cat Limpy had ever seen, and it definitely wasn't nodding its head. It wouldn't even have fitted onto the back shelf of a car.

Suddenly it wasn't slinking any more, it was on top of the lizard doing more crushing and ripping.

Limpy couldn't stop himself, he gave a little whimper.

The jaguar stared in their direction.

Oh no, thought Limpy. It can smell us.

Or rather it could smell Goliath, who'd just let out a large amount of radial-tyre scented wind.

'Quick,' said Limpy. 'Up the tree.'

Goliath looked at him, puzzled.

'Cane toads don't climb trees,' he said.

'We do now,' said Limpy.

16

It was a hard climb up the tree, specially for Limpy with his crook leg. Luckily the bark was covered with ferns and vines and creepers, which were really good for clutching on to and yelling when you thought you were going to fall.

The locals weren't much help. The bark and the stuff hanging off it were full of insects. They obviously didn't like folk climbing over their homes. Not judging by the amount of swearing they did in Limpy and Goliath's direction.

And biting.

And stabbing.

And poison squirting.

'Sorry,' said Limpy to a nest of very annoyed ants. 'We're just trying to escape a killer, ouch, cat.'

He glanced down the tree trunk. No sign of the jaguar, thank swamp. Limpy could just make out, far below on the forest floor, the damp patch that had once been the giant lizard.

'Ow,' said Goliath several hundred times as a swarm of millipedes ran over his face and kicked him in the chin with each of their feet.

Limpy ate a couple of woodlice, just to show them he and Goliath weren't going to be pushed around. They weren't like Australian lice, who generally gave up and accepted things once they were down your throat. Limpy could feel this pair still fighting and kicking after he'd swallowed them.

'Limpy,' said Goliath. 'Why are we still climbing if the big cat's gone?'

'So we can get a better view of the forest,' said Limpy, flicking irate caterpillars out of his eyes with his tongue. 'So we can try and see where Charm and the other cane toads are.'

Goliath didn't reply.

Limpy remembered Goliath didn't like heights.

Oh well, thought Limpy, we're nearly at the top. Then we'll be climbing down. He'll like that better.

'Ow,' said Goliath as a nut bounced off his head.

Limpy looked up. In the branches above them, hairy animals shaped like little humans were hanging by their tails and chucking things.

'Get out of our tree,' yelled one.

'Go back to where you came from,' yelled another.

'Toads don't belong up trees,' yelled a third.

'Except for blood-sucking tree toads,' said another one, peering at Limpy. 'Which you're not.'

Limpy ducked as a lump of bark whizzed past

his ear. He realised something else was whizzing past his ear as well. A brightly coloured bird with a deadly-looking beak. A whole flock of them appeared, circling round Limpy and Goliath, glaring fiercely.

The hairy nut throwers scampered away. Limpy wanted to do the same, but he didn't know how to scamper when he was hanging off a creeper by both hands and his good foot.

'Excuse me,' he said to the birds. 'I'm looking for my relatives. Can you help?'

The birds all laughed.

'What's so funny?' said Goliath indignantly. 'Can you see up my bottom?'

'I think they're telling us there aren't any cane toads up this tree,' said Limpy.

The birds sniggered.

'If you're laughing at my cousin's leg,' yelled Goliath, 'I'll do you.'

One of the birds managed to stop tittering.

'Sorry,' it said. 'We don't mean to be rude. It's just that we've got little parasites in our heads that are eating our brains.'

'Oh,' said Goliath gruffly. 'That's OK then.'

The birds flew off.

Poor things, thought Limpy.

He pulled himself up onto a branch and had a good look round. From up here, near the forest roof, he could see over a much bigger area than down on the ground.

But he couldn't see a single cane toad.

All he could see, on the forest floor and on all the tree trunks and above him in the green canopy, were thousands of creatures trying to hurt and maim and kill each other and eat each other's brains.

Limpy felt sick.

'Charm,' he yelled desperately.

A thousand voices replied, none of them Charm's.

'Come on Goliath,' said Limpy. 'We might as well go back down.'

'I can't,' said Goliath.

Limpy saw that Goliath was clinging to a branch, warts pale with fear.

'Don't make me look down,' said Goliath. 'I can climb up without looking down, but I can't climb down without looking down.'

Limpy hopped onto Goliath's branch, trying to think of something to say to relax him. He saw it wasn't going to be easy. Goliath was showing serious signs of panic. He was chewing his mouthful of rubber sap so fast his jaw was a blur. When Goliath got stressed at home he did the same with human bubblegum he found on the highway.

'Perhaps,' said Limpy, 'you could hang on to me and climb down with your eyes closed.'

Goliath shook his head. His eyes were already closed.

Limpy tried to think of another plan. Then he felt something strange under his feet. He realised the branch they were standing on didn't feel like the other branches, it felt smooth and scaly.

Where narrow beams of sunlight hit the branch it was glinting with different colours.

And moving.

Goliath grabbed Limpy and hung onto him, whimpering. Limpy would have whimpered too if he hadn't been distracted by the sight of a huge head uncoiling from the next tree and glowering at them.

The branch wasn't a branch, it was the biggest snake Limpy had ever seen.

The snake rippled its massive body.

Limpy fought to keep his footing.

He could feel Goliath struggling to do the same.

Unsuccessfully.

Suddenly they were falling, plummeting down through the moist green gloom, the rush of air dragging Limpy's face out of shape.

He gripped Goliath's hand tighter in case it was the last time he had a chance to do it, and prayed that by some miracle they'd land in another human poo farm.

He didn't think they would.

Far below was the forest floor.

Limpy prayed it was bouncy enough to stop two falling toads being splatted into oblivion.

He didn't think it was.

17

While Limpy waited for the fall to end and the forest floor to bash his brains out and probably his spleen as well, he made a wish.

He wished there was another Amazon a bit further down the track. One with a bit less violence and killing. And a bit more ancient knowledge about being friendly.

He wished Charm had gone to that one instead.

Limpy was so busy making his wish he didn't notice at first that he and Goliath weren't falling so fast. It was only when his face went back into shape he realised they were slowing down.

Now he could feel it in his arm too. He was still gripping Goliath's hand, but he wasn't falling any more, he was dangling.

Limpy looked up at Goliath and his face went back out of shape with amazement.

Goliath's eyes were bulging with alarm and his mouth was open in terror. But it wasn't a yell of fear coming out of his mouth, it was a huge rubbery bubble.

Stack me, thought Limpy. Goliath's Amazon bubblegum.

They weren't falling any more, they were floating.

It felt great.

As they drifted down between the mighty trees, Limpy waved to the other floating and gliding creatures around them. They didn't wave back, but Limpy could see that was because they were busy.

A giant long-legged fly with slow-beating silvery wings was busy snatching large spiders off webs and biting them in half.

A furry rat with skin stretched between its back legs was busy gliding into a cloud of poisonous fungus fog.

A shimmering spiral of butterflies floating on the warm air were busy experiencing stomach cramps and wondering if they should be making wills.

Suddenly Limpy didn't feel so great any more.

Even when he and Goliath had landed safely and they'd popped the bubble on a handy twig and Limpy was helping scrape the rubber off Goliath's face, he still didn't feel so great.

The Amazon was a war zone.

'That was fantastic,' said Goliath. 'I feel great.'

'You saved our lives,' said Limpy. 'Thank you.'

'Oh, that was nothing,' said Goliath. 'Saliva and rubber sap. Old commando trick. You can make a tent if you blow hard enough. No, I mean I feel great about this place.'

Goliath gazed around at the forest. He stopped and peered excitedly at something. For a moment Limpy thought Goliath had seen some Amazon rellies, but it was just a battle on a big leaf between an army of ants and an army of termites.

'Look around you,' said Goliath. 'Ancient wisdom all over the place. You can't duck behind a tree for a personal moment without tripping over ancient wisdom. And do you know what this ancient wisdom is saying?'

Limpy had a horrible feeling he did.

'Kill or be killed,' said Goliath, biting the head off a slug so big that even Goliath could only just swallow it. 'Fight or die. Might is right. Survival of the fittest. Strike first and ask questions later. A rolling stone gathers no moss.' Goliath frowned. 'I think that last one might be wrong.'

Limpy didn't reply.

He wanted to tell Goliath the whole thing was wrong. But he couldn't find the words because everything they'd seen since they arrived in the Amazon was saying that Goliath was right.

Limpy made another wish.

That the Amazon rellies would appear now, with Charm, and explain to Goliath why it was much better to live in peace, and how to do it.

They didn't.

'This'd be the place to get an army together,'

Goliath was saying. 'They know how to fight around here.'

He pointed to a tiny beetle on his leg who was trying to crack his shin with its tiny head.

'You're dead, amigo,' said the beetle. 'You're dinner. Just give me a moment.'

'An army from this place would be unstoppable,' said Goliath, eyes shining as he ate the beetle. 'The humans back home wouldn't stand a chance.'

Limpy sighed.

'I suppose that's one good thing about this place,' he said. 'At least we haven't run into any humans.'

'Of course not,' chortled Goliath. 'No humans could survive here.'

A little while later, they ran into some humans.

Or rather the humans ran into them.

Limpy was yelling out Charm's name, hoping perhaps she'd been sleeping and would wake up and hear it. Goliath was chatting to a sloth, admiring the algae growing on its fur.

'Great camouflage,' said Goliath.

The sloth yawned.

'Were you born with it?' asked Goliath. 'Or did you have to plant seeds?'

The sloth yawned again.

Suddenly all the noises of the forest stopped. Limpy's last yell echoed through the trees for a moment, then there was silence.

Except for a faint roaring in the distance.

The sloth went into a panic and clambered up its tree several more centimetres an hour faster than usual.

The roaring was getting louder.

Limpy and Goliath looked at each other. There was something horribly familiar about the sound.

'Big cat,' said Goliath glumly. 'Do we go back up the tree?'

'That's not a cat,' said Limpy. 'That noise is mechanical. Bulldozer mechanical.'

It was so loud now the forest was trembling.

Limpy grabbed Goliath and dragged him into a bog hole, desperately hoping that Amazon bog holes didn't have worms in them that got inside you and opened holiday resorts.

The bulldozers roared and trees crashed down and the ground shook.

Limpy thought it would never stop.

'They work really long shifts around here,' said one of the worms in the bog hole. The other worms agreed. Limpy nodded to show he understood, and that he was grateful the worms were vegetarian.

He stared at the bulldozers and the toppling trees, his warts droopy with despair. So much for peace and friendship. So much for ancient wisdom.

We've come all this way, thought Limpy miserably, and everything's the same. Even the humans' yellow plastic hats are the same. When I finally meet the local cane toads, they'll probably have piles of flat rellies in their bedrooms too.

That's if they haven't already been wiped out.

'Mongrels,' growled Goliath, glaring at the bulldozers. 'Give me a battalion of giant blood-sucking butterflies and I could take them on.'

The worms moved to the other side of the hole.

Finally the bulldozers finished their work and rumbled away.

The forest sounds slowly returned, most of them indignant.

'Go and have a look,' said the worms, pointing to the fallen trees and the scar of dirt the bulldozers had scraped clear. 'It's a disgrace.'

Limpy and Goliath hopped warily over to the clear patch. And saw that it was part of a much bigger bare strip.

They stood in the blinding sunlight, squinting at a massive pipeline that ran along the middle of the strip. The pipeline stretched away to the horizon and, Limpy guessed, beyond. With bare dirt on either side of it all the way.

Goliath hopped over to the pipeline. He wiped up a black smudge with his finger and tasted it.

'Oil,' he called back to Limpy. 'It's a bit spicier than we get on the highway back home, but I'd know the taste anywhere.'

Limpy heard him, but barely took it in.

He'd just seen something on the ground,

half-buried in the freshly gouged dirt, tangled up with the tree roots and creepers and tiny creatures that had been crushed and mangled to death.

Limpy's blood went even colder than usual.

He dragged the thing out and started to brush the dirt off it, making the most desperate wish he'd ever made in his life.

That it would just be a thin length of root, or a very slim dead snake.

But it wasn't.

It was woven from spiders' web, with dried mouse eyes threaded on it.

Charm's necklace.

18

The sun burned into Limpy's back as he searched for Charm's body.

He didn't care.

It was nowhere near as painful as the anger he felt inside when he pictured those humans in their bulldozers crushing poor little Charm.

'Is this a bit of her?' asked Goliath miserably.

He held up a scrap of warty skin.

Limpy looked.

It wasn't Charm.

For an angry moment he thought it might be human skin. A bulldozer driver who'd been to a beauty parlour to get some warts. And then fallen under his own bulldozer while he admired himself in the side mirror.

But it wasn't that either.

'It's a lizard,' said Limpy. 'Those aren't warts, they're wheel track marks.'

'Mongrel humans,' muttered Goliath. 'When I

106

get my hands on them, they're dead.'

Limpy didn't argue.

They kept on searching until the sun started to sink behind the trees.

'This is hopeless,' said Goliath. 'I don't reckon we're ever gunna find her.'

Limpy knew Goliath was right. They'd have no chance in the dark.

'I can smell water over there,' said Goliath. 'Come on, let's get some mud on our sunburn.'

As Limpy followed, the air started to feel cooler on his aching body.

But inside him nothing felt cooler at all.

Limpy sat on the riverbank, staring at the blood-red water.

As the sunset faded, night creatures started to appear.

A moth sat trembling on a branch overhanging the river. At first Limpy assumed the moth had heard about Charm and was in a rage too. Then he remembered that moths had to shiver for a while to get their wing muscles warm enough to fly.

Before the moth could take off, a fish leapt out of the water and gulped it down.

Limpy watched as the fish sped away, sending ripples out across the surface of the water.

A shadow passed over Limpy. A large bat had spotted the ripples and was swinging round in mid-flight. It came in low over the river, dipped its claws into the water, snatched up the fish and disappeared into the dark tree tops.

Soon, in the moonlight, the water was a frenzy of activity.

Shoals of fish with gleaming razor teeth tore into eels, crabs, prawns and, if they couldn't find anything else, each other.

Stingrays grappled with giant turtles.

Otters bigger than human eskies took chunks out of catfish bigger than humans.

Limpy watched it all and nodded grimly.

Goliath's right, he thought. This is the way of the world. Kill or be killed. Fight or perish. An eye for an eye.

Limpy flexed his glands as a flying beetle with razor-sharp jaws hurtled towards him.

I wish I'd understood this before, thought Limpy as he hit the beetle full in the face with a perfectly aimed droplet of poison pus.

But I do now.

Limpy found Goliath nearby in the forest, trying to train an army.

'Atten-shun,' yelled Goliath.

Several rows of termites stood to attention in the thin streams of moonlight, but a large column of ants ignored him and started eating the termites.

'At ease,' yelled Goliath.

A platoon of ticks stood at ease on the belly of

a small furry animal, but a squadron of bats swooped down and the ticks dived for cover.

'Face the front,' yelled Goliath.

The bats formed a wobbly line. Limpy could see Goliath's problem. As well as trying to stay in parade-ground formation, the bats were also sucking the furry animal's blood out through the tick bites.

'No,' yelled Goliath. 'Hopeless. What was I saying before about discipline? It's not enough being perfectly formed killing machines. If you lot are gunna wipe humans off the face of the planet, you need discipline. And bombs, but we'll talk about that later.'

Limpy tapped Goliath on the shoulder.

'Sorry to interrupt,' he said. 'I need some military advice.'

'Shoot,' said Goliath.

A raiding party of highly-toxic caterpillars raised their barb-bristling thoraxes into firing position.

'Not you,' said Goliath.

'Make up your mind,' said the caterpillars, lowering their thoraxes.

'Goliath,' said Limpy. 'If an individual was going to do a commando attack against the humans, inflicting as much damage as possible, where would be the best place to do it?'

'You mean,' said Goliath, 'what's their weak spot?'

Limpy nodded.

'Oil,' said Goliath. 'They can't exist without it. You've seen them on the highway at home. Without oil they'd be carrying those cars on their backs.'

A platoon of turtles thought this was hilarious.

'Silence,' yelled Goliath.

The turtles ignored him.

'The great thing about oil,' said Goliath, glaring at the turtles, 'is that if you set fire to it, it burns really well. If you're lucky, it explodes.'

Limpy remembered the oil pipeline they'd seen earlier that day.

'Thanks,' he said. 'That's exactly what I wanted to know.'

'You're welcome,' said Goliath. 'Sharing information and working together, that's the way to win a war.'

He looked meaningfully at the bats, who were still sucking.

Goliath's right, thought Limpy grimly as he hopped away.

That's exactly what this is.

War.

19

Limpy had to wait until morning before he could attack because he needed the sun to blow up the oil pipeline.

'Ow,' said the butterfly who was helping him. 'That sun's hot.'

'Sorry,' said Limpy. 'But that's the whole point.'

'Explain it again,' said the butterfly.

Limpy explained again how if there was a highway nearby with broken headlights on it like at home, he could use the glass to focus the sun's rays and ignite the oil. But because there wasn't, the wings of a transparent butterfly were the next best thing.

'Why do you have to fold them?' complained the butterfly. 'When I agreed to help you, you didn't say anything about folding.'

'Doubles the magnification,' said Limpy. 'Won't be long now. Just think of your poor dead family members, crushed by those bulldozers.'

The butterfly did that.

'Heartless brutes,' it sobbed.

Limpy thought about his poor dead family member and her lovely smile that he'd never see again.

It helped him concentrate on focussing the sun's rays onto the oil stains. They were seeping out of what he was pretty sure was a pumping station. He could hear a rhythmic wheezing under the cracked metal cover that sounded exactly like Goliath's chest when Goliath tried to suck the petrol out of parked cars through their exhaust pipes.

'How are we going?' said the butterfly.

'Nearly there,' said Limpy.

The oil under the sunspot was starting to smoke. Once it burst into flames, Limpy planned to dive for cover with the butterfly while fire roared down the inside of the pipeline all the way to some distant city. Where hopefully it would set off a huge explosion destroying everything around it and teaching those mongrel humans to think twice before they killed any more innocent little sisters.

'Stop,' said a loud voice. 'Stop, for swamp's sake.'

It wasn't the butterfly.

Limpy spun round and got such a shock his mucus started wobbling even though the sun had dried it almost solid.

Cane toads.

A large group of them, hurrying towards him, alarmed expressions on their faces.

Stack me, thought Limpy. Amazon rellies.

The one at the front, who was even bigger than Goliath and a lot more noble-looking, hopped over to the pumping station and peed onto the smoking oil.

'Hey,' said Limpy angrily. 'It took us ages to get that started.'

'That's right,' said the butterfly, wincing as it straightened out its wings. 'I may never feature in a television nature documentary again.'

Limpy wished Goliath was here instead of in the forest teaching stink beetles how to march. He'd put these dumb rellies in their place.

The big cane toad looked down at Limpy with a stern expression.

'Do you have any idea what would have happened if you'd set that oil alight?' he said.

'Yes,' said Limpy. 'I do.'

'You want war with the humans?' said the cane toad, glancing at the other cane toads in disbelief.

'Yes,' said Limpy. 'I do.'

'Well, we don't,' said the cane toad. 'We've got enough enemies in the forest as it is. Every second living thing around here wants to either eat us, drown us, grow fungus on us, use us as flooring material in a nest or take our brains out and let their kids play in our skulls. The last thing we want is humans after us as well.'

For a fleeting moment, Limpy was tempted to ask the rellies what their secret was for keeping humans off their backs.

Then he remembered he didn't care any more.

All he cared about was avenging Charm.

'The mongrel humans killed my sister,' said Limpy.

The big cane toad looked at Limpy, his face softening.

'I see,' he said. 'I'm sorry.'

The other cane toads looked pretty sympathetic too. For a moment Limpy thought they were going to leave him alone so he could get back to blowing up humans.

No such luck.

'These tragedies happen,' said the big cane toad. 'Some of us have lost loved ones too. Just a few, fortunately. It's a big forest. We stay away from the humans and hope they stay away from us.'

Is that it? thought Limpy bitterly. Is that the ancient wisdom Charm gave her life for? That's pathetic. We could have stayed at home and worked that out for ourselves. Even Goliath could.

'Are you from the other side of the river?' asked the cane toad.

'Australia,' muttered Limpy.

The other cane toads looked puzzled.

'I've heard of Australia,' said the big cane toad. 'A bird told me about it. Incredible place. The only things that kill toads there are humans, right?'

Limpy nodded, wishing the whole crowd of them would hop off and squirt bugs or something.

The big cane toad put his arm round Limpy's shoulders.

'I'm Raoul,' he said. 'I'd like to hear more about Australia, and you look like you could do with a drink and some moisturiser on those warts. Come back to our swamp. Be our guest.'

It was a kind offer, but Limpy wasn't interested.

As Raoul steered him away from the pipeline towards the forest, Limpy came up with a desperate plan.

Push Raoul over, elbow the other cane toads out of the way, hop back to the pipeline, grab another see-through butterfly and get the oil alight before they caught up with him.

Limpy took a deep breath, then flung himself at Raoul.

He'd tried to push Goliath over a few times, so he knew it wasn't going to be easy. But Goliath was a floppy sack of wombat guts compared to Raoul, whose muscles felt like steel bridge cables as Limpy bounced off them.

Caught by surprise, Raoul staggered backwards.

Limpy turned and started hopping as fast as he could, praying his crook leg wouldn't send him on a curve into the river.

He needn't have worried.

Before he'd done two hops, Limpy felt Raoul's powerful hand on his shoulder. His legs, even his good one, weren't nearly strong enough to propel him out of Raoul's firm but gentle grip.

'I'm sorry,' said Raoul. 'I know how you feel. But I have to insist you be our guest.'

Limpy didn't bother struggling.

Pretty soon Goliath would be here to rescue him.

Then, thought Limpy, we'll ditch these wimps and get back to our war.

20

Come on, Goliath, thought Limpy. I'm sick of waiting. Come and rescue me.

Limpy lifted his head from the pillow of leaves and peered through the forest gloom.

No sign of Goliath.

In the distance Limpy could just make out Raoul and the other cane toads at the edge of their swamp, having a fight with a swarm of giant wasps. The Amazon rellies were obviously crack shots with their poison glands. The wasps were copping it bad.

Please, Goliath, thought Limpy. This is the perfect time to rescue me. While those wimps are all walloping wasps.

Still no sign of Goliath.

For the millionth time Limpy tried to wriggle out of the creeper knotted around him. No good. Raoul had tied it too tight.

'Mongrel,' muttered Limpy.

He was so angry with Raoul he decided not to feel grateful that Raoul had placed little pads of moss wherever the creeper would have cut into his skin.

Limpy scowled at the distant cane toads.

He wasn't impressed by the Amazon rellies' squirting skills either. All he wanted to do was get back to what was really important.

Blowing up humans.

If Raoul was a real fighter, thought Limpy grimly, he'd know that commandos don't rest till the war's won. And if he was a real rellie, he'd help me avenge Charm.

'Pssst.'

Limpy looked up and saw a familiar face peering at him out of a tangle of leaves some distance away.

Goliath.

At last.

Limpy's warts tingled with relief.

From the wavy mud streaks on Goliath's face and the way his bottom lip was jutting out, Limpy could tell he was planning a daring rescue.

Except why wasn't Goliath coming over?

Perhaps he's got slug juice in his eyes, thought Limpy, and he's not sure if it's me.

'Goliath,' whispered Limpy. 'It's me. Over here.'

But Goliath stayed crouched in the under-growth. His put a finger to his lips and glanced around the forest.

Then he started doing hand signals. Big complicated ones that went on for ages. At first Limpy thought Goliath was saying he had burrowing worms in his armpits and was planning to try and smoke them out using the sun and see-through butterflies.

'Later,' whispered Limpy. 'After we've set fire to the oil.'

Goliath shook his head and repeated the hand signal. This time Limpy recognised it. It was the gesture Aunty Pru had given Goliath the time she was teaching philosophy to Charm, and Goliath wanted her to watch how swallowing dragonflies made his tummy ripple.

'Be patient,' the hand signal said. 'I'll be with you in a while.'

A while? thought Limpy. Why not now?

'Goliath,' said Limpy. 'Untie me now.'

Goliath tried a new hand signal.

'You're going for a swim?' exploded Limpy. 'You can't go for a swim now.'

Limpy saw Goliath frown, then give up on the hand signals.

'Hang on, Limpy,' croaked Goliath. 'I'm training a special rescue unit to rescue you. They're coming along well for raw jungle recruits, and as soon as they stop eating each other, in a day or two at the most, we'll be coming to liberate you. Hang on.'

'Goliath,' hissed Limpy. 'Get over here. The

Amazon rellies aren't watching. You don't need a special rescue unit.'

But Goliath had slipped away into the jungle, leaving only a trembling leaf and a glob of mucus with half a maggot in it to show he'd ever been there.

Limpy's warts felt like they were about to explode with frustration.

He glared back over at the Amazon rellies, still busy blasting wasps.

Goliath could have used a chainsaw to cut the knots and they wouldn't have noticed.

'Look at that lot,' hissed a voice from somewhere very close. 'Are we Amazon toads good squirters, or what?'

Limpy looked round, startled. It wasn't Goliath's voice.

A cane toad appeared from behind a clump of reeds.

Limpy tried not to stare. The cane toad was about the same size as him, and about the same age, and had exactly the same squashed leg.

Stack me, thought Limpy.

He'd seen plenty of cane toads with squashed bits, including squashed heads which this bloke had as well. But he'd never seen anyone with exactly the same squashed leg.

'Do you agree?' said the cane toad. 'That Amazon toads are good fighters?'

He gave Limpy either a smile or a scowl. Limpy

couldn't be sure because the poor bloke's face was almost flat on one side.

Limpy nodded, partly because it was true and partly because he felt sorry for a person who couldn't even let other people know if he was happy or angry.

'You're right, we are good fighters,' said the cane toad. 'Trouble is, we're fighting the wrong enemy. We should be fighting the slimy murderous black-hearted pimply humans.'

Limpy stared at him.

The other cane toad's expression was still hard to work out. Except for his eyes. They were glinting with so much dark hatred they made Limpy shiver.

With delight.

'I agree,' said Limpy.

'I know you do,' said the cane toad. 'Wait here. I've got something that will help us do it.'

Limpy strained hopelessly against the creeper knotted around him.

'I'm not going anywhere,' he said.

The very squashed cane toad hopped away into the undergrowth, leaning over a bit so he didn't go into a curve.

Amazing, thought Limpy. He even hops like me.

Soon he reappeared.

Limpy saw he was holding something wet wrapped in a leaf.

The cane toad looked around furtively, checking

that the other cane toads were still busy in the distance, and sidled over to Limpy.

'My name is Flatface,' he said. 'Do you know why?'

Limpy didn't want to hurt his feelings.

'Um . . . because . . . because you always face the street, like a block of flats?'

As soon as Limpy said it, he felt like kicking himself in the bum. An Amazon cane toad probably wouldn't even know what a street was. Or a block of flats.

Flatface didn't seem to have noticed.

'When I was little, a human bulldozer did this,' he said, pointing to his face and leg. 'If I hadn't seen the bulldozer at the last moment, it would have killed me.'

'Murdering mongrels,' said Limpy.

'I lay in the mud,' continued Flatface. 'Crushed, broken, with insects laughing at me. That's when I vowed revenge on the human species.'

Limpy felt his throat sac tighten.

'I've spent my life planning that revenge,' continued Flatface. 'And now I'm ready. Except those fools over there won't give me the help I need.'

Flatface glared across the swamp at the other cane toads, then held the leaf parcel out to Limpy.

'This is the sap of three different jungle vines,' he said. 'Mixed together it makes a powerful poison. A tiny amount will kill many humans.'

Limpy stared at the parcel. This was it. Precious ancient knowledge. And it was being handed to him on a leaf.

'It needs one more ingredient,' said Flatface. 'Our poison, from our glands. But my glands were crushed. And those idiots won't give me any poison because they're too gutless and wartless to start a war with humans.'

Limpy felt his own glands tingling.

Flatface was staring at him, dark eyes big with hatred.

'You and I,' said Flatface, 'working together, can kill many, many humans.'

He started undoing the knots that were holding Limpy.

'Do you like that idea?' he asked softly.

Limpy thought of poor Charm lying under a human bulldozer. Maybe even suffering insect jeers before she died.

He nodded.

He did like that idea.

He liked it very much.

Despite his crook leg, Flatface was a fast hopper. By the time they arrived at the ditch, Limpy was out of breath. So when Flatface pointed out the first lot of humans they were going to kill, Limpy knew why he wasn't feeling quite as joyful about it as he should.

It's because I'm pooped, thought Limpy.

He gasped in some more air through his pores. Then he peered over the edge of the ditch again at the humans in the village.

No, he still wasn't tingling with delight and revenge. In fact he was starting to have a bad feeling.

Limpy looked at Flatface, wondering how he was going to break the news.

'They're the wrong ones,' he said.

'What do you mean?' said Flatface.

'The wrong humans,' said Limpy.

'No they're not,' said Flatface. 'We're here to kill humans and these are humans. Look, two legs, horrible smooth skin, runny noses most of them. But not for long. When we add our little surprise to their drinking water, they won't be doing any more running, not them or their noses.'

'There's been a misunderstanding,' said Limpy. 'This isn't what I was expecting.'

These humans weren't on bulldozers. There wasn't a single one wearing a hard hat or overalls. Most of them weren't wearing anything at all. They were strolling around the village chatting, or sitting playing with children.

Limpy stared at a mum and dad dangling their little kid upside down by his feet.

Mum and Dad used to do that to me, thought Limpy. When I swallowed a snail without peeling it first.

Deep in his guts the bad feeling got bigger.

It wasn't an unpeeled snail, it was something else.

'What were you expecting?' said Flatface. 'Oh, I get it. Larger numbers, right? Look, don't worry, we're starting small to test the dosage, but then we'll move on to bigger groups.'

Limpy tried to nod. He wanted to agree, for Charm's sake, but something inside him was saying no.

'Look at them,' said Flatface, scowling at the humans. 'Innocent laughing faces. You wouldn't guess how murderous their brains are, would you? Nature can be very dishonest sometimes.'

Limpy tried to imagine each one of these humans on a bulldozer, ruthlessly destroying trees, making sandwich-spread out of the forest, driving over Charm.

He couldn't.

'Come on,' said Flatface, unwrapping the leaf parcel. 'Let's have a squirt of your pus in here and we're in business.'

Limpy stared at the houses around the edge of the village. They were made from twigs and dried leaves and looked small and friendly compared to the human houses back home. Limpy tried to persuade himself that inside each one was a bulldozer or a truck or a pile of really sharp pie crusts.

He couldn't.

'I can't,' he said.

Before Flatface could stop him, Limpy flung himself out of the ditch and hopped back into the forest as fast as he could.

He just wanted to be on his own, to think about Charm and trucks and bulldozers, to smash through the undergrowth like this with thorny vines slashing his face.

To feel angry again.

It didn't happen.

Flatface grabbed him from behind.

'That's not fair,' yelled Limpy as he struggled in Flatface's grasp. 'Your leg is just as crook as mine. How come you can hop faster? How come you're stronger?'

'Ancient Amazon health diet,' said a nearby scorpion. 'And he broods a lot.'

Then something even more unfair happened.

Flatface dragged Limpy over to a large pit dug deep into the forest floor and pushed him in.

Luckily the damp leaves on the bottom were soft and as Limpy thudded into them his warts were only dented rather than completely flattened.

When Limpy's head stopped thumping, he squinted up. Flatface was glaring down at him over the edge of the pit. He looked pretty small, and Limpy knew that meant one of two things.

Either Flatface had shrunk, or the mouth of the pit was a long way up.

Limpy wished he'd paid a bit more attention in the maths lessons Dad had tried to give him, instead of spending most of the time gazing longingly at the mud slide. He had a horrible feeling the correct answer was the second one.

'Gone shy about squirting pus, eh?' said Flatface. 'I think you'll change your mind when you meet your new friends down there. I'll be back later to collect it. Bye.'

He disappeared.

I wonder what he means by new friends, thought Limpy. Probably not cane toads who like mud slides.

The answer came from the other end of the pit. It started with some loud hissing, followed by quite a lot of slithering and the sudden appearance of several pairs of red and yellow eyes staring at Limpy.

'G'day,' said Limpy. 'Um, are you those giant caterpillars Raoul was telling me about? The ones that can inflate your bodies to look like big snakes?'

'No,' said a grumpy voice. 'We're snakes who can fluff our scales out to look like very poisonous giant caterpillars. That's why humans dig pits to catch us. They like to watch us do it.'

'Oh,' said Limpy. 'I see. And er, do you um, eat cane toads?'

'No,' said the grumpy voice. 'Not eat. Any more questions before we suck your insides out and use your skin for bedding?'

'Not really,' said Limpy.

The question he wanted to ask someone was whether he should spray the snakes to defend himself and risk some of his poison pus falling into the hands of Flatface.

It probably wasn't worth asking the snakes that.

To make conversation, Limpy was about to ask the snakes if by any chance they fancied joining him in a war against humans on bulldozers, when something prodded him in the back.

It was a stick.

A very long stick, held by someone leaning over the edge of the pit.

Limpy stared up.

It was a human kid, one of the boys he'd seen

128

playing in the village. He recognised the coloured stripes painted on the boy's chest.

Trembling, Limpy waited for the boy to stab him.

It was what some human boys did, he'd heard about it loads of times around the swamp at home. Either that or blow you up with bike pumps. They did it to pass the time while they were waiting to grow up into bulldozer drivers.

Bye Goliath, thought Limpy sadly. I'm glad you're not here.

But the boy didn't stab him, he just prodded Limpy gently and gestured until Limpy realised the boy wanted him to hang onto the stick so he could lift him out of the pit.

Limpy hung on.

Probably wants to stab me up top where he can see better, thought Limpy as he travelled up and the snakes muttered bitterly below.

Perhaps Flatface was right about humans after all.

But the boy didn't stab Limpy up top.

He spoke gently to Limpy in a language Limpy didn't understand, then carried him through the forest, put him down at the edge of the swamp, grinned, waved goodbye, and disappeared into the bushes leaving Limpy feeling very confused.

22

While Limpy dug a grave on the riverbank, he had a long think.

He thought about humans, and how cruel some of them were, and how kind others of them were, and how confusing that was.

He thought about Flatface, and wondered if Flatface ever got confused.

But mostly he thought about Charm and all her special qualities.

The way she could make slugs laugh, even while Goliath was eating them.

The way she let smaller kids go before her on the mud slide, even though at least one of them always did a poo in the mud from excitement.

The way she always said sorry if she lost her temper and tried to stab you with a mosquito.

'Oh, Charm,' whispered Limpy. 'I miss you.'

He wished he could do that thing humans did with their eyes when they were sad, because it seemed to make them feel better.

Instead he picked up Charm's necklace and looked at it sorrowfully. After a while he noticed that the dried mouse eyes seemed to be looking back at him just as sorrowfully.

'You got a bit carried away back there, didn't you?' they seemed to be saying. They seemed to be saying it in Aunty Pru's voice.

Limpy nodded.

'You're right,' he said. 'I did. I wanted to kill every human in the world. And that was a mistake. I should have just tried to kill every human that has ever driven a bulldozer or built a bulldozer or sold a bulldozer or repaired a bulldozer or cleaned the condensation off the inside of the windscreen of a bulldozer.'

'And how would that have made you feel?' asked Aunty Pru's voice in Limpy's head.

'Great,' said Limpy. 'Even better than beating Uncle George at mucus-twirling.'

Inside Limpy, Aunty Pru seemed to sigh.

Limpy realised it wasn't her, it was him.

'But I wouldn't have felt great for long,' said Limpy quietly. 'Because Charm would still be dead. And so would you, Aunty Pru.'

Aunty Pru's voice didn't say anything.

It didn't have to.

Limpy knew that if she was here, she'd be smiling at him sadly and nodding.

He held the necklace for a moment more, then

kissed it and dropped it into the empty grave. He covered it over and gently patted the soil with his hands.

'Bye, Charm,' he whispered. 'I'm going to finish our quest.'

Then he went to find Goliath.

Goliath was in the forest, having trouble with his special rescue unit.

'No,' he was yelling at a platoon of ribbon worms. 'You do not march like that. Marching is keeping in step. If you don't keep in step, it's not marching.'

'But we can't keep in step,' said one of the ribbon worms.

'How many times do I have to tell you?' yelled Goliath. 'Call me sir. We can't keep in step, sir. Anyway, why can't you keep in step? Give me one good reason?'

'We haven't got feet, sir,' said the ribbon worm.

'This is pathetic,' roared Goliath. 'At this rate my cousin's going to be a prisoner for the rest of his life.'

Limpy tapped Goliath on the shoulder.

'Goliath,' he said. 'It's OK. I'm free. Now we can get on with our quest.'

Goliath sighed crossly, glaring at the ribbon worms. 'Limpy, not now,' he said. 'I'm trying to train a rescue unit. Stack me, look at that. Those butterflies haven't got the faintest idea how to crawl through the mud on their bellies.'

'Goliath,' said Limpy. 'I'm free.'

'Call yourself a special rescue unit?' Goliath was yelling at the butterflies. 'It's pathetic.'

Then Goliath spun round and stared at Limpy, his big warty face lighting up with amazement and delight.

'Limpy,' he croaked. 'You're free.'

The ribbon worms and butterflies all applauded.

Limpy gripped Goliath's arm.

'Come on,' he said. 'We've wasted enough time. We've got to get back to searching for the ancient secret of friendship with humans.'

Goliath was looking doubtful.

'What about blowing up the bulldozers?' he said. 'And the bulldozer drivers' lunchboxes?'

Limpy took a deep breath. It wouldn't be fair to get cross with Goliath. Not after all the effort he'd put into training his rescue unit.

'There are other humans here,' said Limpy. 'In a village. One of them rescued me. The others look pretty friendly too. I think we might be getting closer to the ancient secret.'

Goliath was still looking doubtful.

'We didn't come here for war,' said Limpy. 'We came here for peace. Charm lost her life for this quest and that's why we're going to carry on till we succeed. For Charm.'

'All right,' said Goliath, looking sad and a bit

ashamed. 'But after we've succeeded, we'll do the war.'

Limpy decided the time had come to get cross with Goliath.

Before he could, he felt a hand on his shoulder.

Limpy looked up. It was Raoul. There was hurt and anger on Raoul's big face. Limpy decided not to waste time with excuses.

'I'm sorry I escaped,' said Limpy. 'And I'm sorry I tried to start a war.'

Raoul's frown got even deeper.

Goliath thrust himself between Limpy and Raoul.

'It wasn't his fault,' said Goliath. 'It was me. I rescued him with my highly trained rescue unit. I'm the one you should be crook with.'

Limpy saw Goliath notice Raoul's muscles. Goliath reached out and gave one of them a little tweak. And felt how hard it was.

'Not too crook, but,' he said, shrinking back.

'I'm not just angry with you two,' said Raoul. 'I'm angry with Flatface. And with myself for letting him get near you. Two warmongers working together could have been a disaster.'

'Three,' said Goliath indignantly.

'I'm sorry, Raoul,' said Limpy. 'I shouldn't have tried to blow up the pipeline. I got carried away, but I'm over it now. Me and Goliath and Charm came here to discover your ancient secret of living in peace with humans, and that's what I want to do.'

Raoul's angry frown turned into a surprised one.

'Our ancient secret?' he said. He thought for a moment. 'I don't think we've got an ancient secret. I've never heard of one.'

Limpy stared at Raoul, struggling to take this in.

'The humans in the village,' said Limpy. 'They don't kill cane toads, do they? They don't drive over them in vehicles or bash them with cricket bats or blow them up with bike pumps.'

'No,' said Raoul. 'I don't think so.'

'Why not?' said Limpy.

'Don't know,' said Raoul. 'Never really thought about it. We've always been more concerned about wasps and snakes and eagles and giant ticks.'

Limpy felt his warts droop with despair.

'There is someone who might know,' said Raoul. 'We have a wise ancient being among us who knows the secrets of the forest. Secrets of dreams and magic. When he closes his eyes, nothing is hidden from him. He'd probably know.'

Limpy's mucus wobbled with excitement.

'Thank you,' said Limpy. 'Thank you. Where can we find this wise ancient toad?'

Raoul looked at Limpy with a rather nervous expression.

'He's not a toad,' said Raoul. 'He's a human.'

Limpy and Goliath crouched in the ditch at the edge of the human village.

'Let me get this straight,' said Goliath. 'We're not attacking them.'

'No,' said Limpy.

'Not even a little bit.'

'No.'

Goliath frowned. 'But if we're not attacking them,' he said, 'how are we going to capture the wise bloke who can tell us the ancient secret?'

Limpy sighed.

Goliath's face lit up.

'I get it,' he said. 'We're going in undercover to kidnap him, right? Good plan. What shall we disguise ourselves as? Giant snakes? Bulldozers? Sheep?'

'Goliath,' said Limpy. 'We're not using violence and we're not using trickery. We're just going in there politely, and when we work out which is the wise old man, we'll ask him to tell us the secret.'

Goliath stared at Limpy.

'Are you mental?' he said. 'Walking into a human village in broad daylight? What if they throw spears at us? Or fire poison darts at us? Or hollow us out and use us as drinking vessels?'

Part of Limpy felt the same as Goliath.

Compared to what they were about to do, hanging out in a pit full of snakes didn't seem that scary after all.

But another part of him was prepared to take the risk.

For Charm's sake.

'My poison sacs are empty,' wailed Goliath. 'I used them up this morning in a military training exercise. I'm defenceless. What if the humans flatten us to make trays for their TV dinners?'

Limpy opened his pores and took a deep breath and tried to stop his mucus from trembling.

'We'll just have to trust they don't,' he said.

So far, thought Limpy, so good.

He and Goliath were in the village, and so far not a single spear or dart or scooping-out tool had been aimed at them.

Only looks.

Every eye in the village was watching them. Men humans, women humans, kid humans.

'Keep hopping,' said Limpy.

He was glad Goliath's poison sacs were empty.

When Goliath got scared he tended to squirt first and ask questions later.

'You should have let me bring back-up troops,' muttered Goliath. 'Just the sight of a thousand highly trained troops would have had those humans running for their lives.'

'Goliath,' said Limpy. 'Apart from the fact that we're trying to be friendly, I don't think anyone's going to be particularly scared by the sight of a thousand highly trained troops eating each other.'

Goliath sighed.

'You're right,' he said. 'I'm a hopeless army general. If we get out of this alive, I'm going to give the army away. Try a completely different approach with humans.'

'That's good,' said Limpy. 'I'm glad to hear it.'

'I'm gunna start a navy,' said Goliath. 'Fire missiles at humans from the middle of the swamp.'

Limpy was about to sigh, but suddenly he needed his breath for something more urgent.

A gasp of alarm.

Two human women carrying large pots were coming over, blocking the way. Limpy stopped hopping. So did Goliath. The women bent over them and smiled.

Goliath hopped behind Limpy.

'Please,' he whimpered. 'Don't put us in those pots. We're mostly gristle and blubber. Let us live and I'll drop the idea of the navy, honest.'

'Hi there, fellas,' said a voice. 'You lost?'

Limpy wasn't sure who was speaking at first. He knew it couldn't be the women because he could understand the language. Then he saw a tiny monkey peeking out from the hair of one of the women.

'If I can help you with anything,' said the monkey, 'ask away.'

'Doesn't that human mind you being in her hair?' said Limpy.

'I'd watch out if she sees you,' said Goliath to the monkey. 'Hairy little tyke like you would make a great toilet brush.'

'She likes having me here,' said the monkey, chewing happily. 'I eat all the insects that get caught in her hair.'

Limpy stared.

Perhaps this was a clue.

Perhaps the secret of living in peace with humans had something to do with being useful.

'Here to see anyone in particular?' asked the monkey.

'We've come to see the ancient wise man,' said Limpy.

'Over there,' said the monkey. 'Second hut on the right.'

'Thanks,' said Limpy.

While he and Goliath hopped towards the hut, Limpy glanced around at the humans, who were all still watching.

Most of them were smiling.

'This is great,' said Limpy. 'But it's a bit unusual. I wonder why all these humans are being so friendly. I mean, we're cane toads.

'I was wondering that too,' said Goliath. 'I think it must be our very special personalities.'

24

Inside the hut everything was dark and smoky.

Limpy could see the shape of the ancient human sitting on the ground.

'Welcome,' said a voice in language Limpy understood. 'Come in.'

Limpy and Goliath hopped towards the figure.

That's good, thought Limpy. The ancient human must have a monkey in his hair too. Perhaps the monkey can help us explain to him why we're here.

But as they got closer, Limpy saw that the ancient human didn't have a monkey in his hair. He didn't even have any hair, his head was completely bald. And there was no monkey hiding in his clothes because he wasn't wearing any.

'What can I do for you?' said the voice.

Limpy stared.

The voice was coming from the ancient human's mouth.

Stack me, thought Limpy. A human's speaking to me and I can understand everything he's saying.

Goliath was looking amazed too.

'He must have a monkey halfway down his throat eating cough germs,' he muttered.

'Don't be alarmed,' said the ancient human. 'I speak your language. In ancient times all humans and animals spoke the same language. Then humans developed languages of their own. It was so they could swap recipes without their dinner overhearing and getting nervous.'

Limpy was impressed. This ancient human really did possess ancient wisdom.

The old man smiled and winked at them.

'Have you got something in your eye?' said Goliath. 'I've got some mucus here that's really good for getting grit out.'

'No thanks,' said the ancient human. 'I'm fine. But you're obviously not or you wouldn't have come to see me.'

Limpy opened his mouth to explain their quest, but before he could start he saw something so amazing, so incredible that the words jammed in his throat.

Hanging on the wall behind the ancient human was a necklace.

Charm's necklace.

Limpy leapt past the old man, snatched the necklace off its hook and examined it more closely.

It was identical to the one Aunty Pru had given

Charm. Woven from spider's web with dried mouse eyes threaded on it.

Limpy was about to demand to know what Charm's necklace was doing there when he saw something even more amazing and incredible.

Hanging on other hooks on the wall were other necklaces.

Exactly the same as the one in his hand.

Limpy struggled to speak.

'These . . . these necklaces. Where did you get them?'

The ancient human gave a gentle smile. 'They're traditional,' he said. 'Folk around here have been wearing them since time began.'

Limpy struggled to take this in.

'Are there many of them?' he asked.

'Yes,' said the ancient human. 'Everyone's got them. I've got six.'

Suddenly Limpy's mind was racing.

The necklace he'd found in the mud.

Perhaps it wasn't Charm's.

Perhaps she wasn't dead.

Limpy saw that the ancient human was watching him, still smiling.

'The necklace you found was one of mine,' said the ancient human. 'I hung it on a bulldozer to try and remind the driver that his ancestors came from this forest.'

Limpy stared at the ancient human.

He wanted to shout with joy. He wanted to

swing from the roof rafters and beat his chest and yodel with joy.

Instead he grabbed Goliath.

'Those necklaces,' Goliath was saying with a frown. 'I've seen one of those somewhere before.'

'Goliath,' said Limpy. 'Charm's not dead. The necklace I found in the clearing wasn't hers.'

Goliath stared at him, the news slowly sinking in.

'Where is she?' he said.

'I don't know,' said Limpy.

He pictured Charm somewhere in the jungle, lost and scared, with monkeys throwing things at her and jaguars stalking her and insects trying to lay eggs under her warts.

He felt dizzy with worry, and joy, and more worry.

The ancient human gave another soft smile. 'I know where she is,' he said.

Limpy stared at him.

'Where?' croaked Limpy. He could hear Goliath croaking it too.

'You love your sister very much, don't you?' said the ancient human.

'Yes,' said Limpy. 'I do.'

'So do I,' said Goliath. 'That time I put a tickle bug in her bed was just a practical joke.'

'Twenty-seven tickle bugs, wasn't it?' said the ancient human.

Goliath stared at him.

So did Limpy.

How did he know that?

'Your sister came to see me this morning,' said the ancient human. 'I told her you were both in the jungle and I told her where to find you.'

'But she didn't find us,' said Limpy.

'That's because,' said the ancient human, 'after I sent her, you left to come here.'

'So where is she now?' said Limpy.

'Give me a moment,' said the ancient human.

He took a very deep breath and closed his eyes. And stayed that way for what seemed to Limpy like much longer than a moment.

'I think he's asleep,' said Goliath. 'Shall I tickle his foot with a bit of mucus?'

Limpy shook his head. 'Raoul reckons this bloke can see everything in the forest,' he whispered. 'Without leaving his hut.'

Many more moments passed.

Limpy was getting concerned.

The ancient human didn't seem to be breathing.

What if the effort of trying to see everything in the forest had been too much for him?

What if he'd died?

Not only would Charm never be found, but the humans might blame Limpy and Goliath for over-stressing their wise ancient leader and a war might break out between the forest humans and the forest toads for the first time since time began.

The ancient human opened his eyes.

145

'Your sister is safe and well,' he said. 'I'll draw you a map.'

He started drawing in the dust at his feet.

'Thank you,' said Limpy, weak with relief. 'Thank you so much. How can I ever repay you?'

'Well,' said the ancient human, 'you could do a pee in that pot.'

He pointed to a pot similar to the ones the women outside had been carrying.

Limpy was confused.

'Are you sure?' he said to the ancient human. 'Isn't that a drinking water pot?'

'Yes,' said the ancient human. 'That's why I'd be grateful if you could pee in it.'

Limpy looked at Goliath.

Perhaps the strain of locating Charm had been too much for the ancient human's brain.

'I'll do it,' said Goliath, hopping up onto the rim of the pot.

'Actually,' said the ancient human, 'Just your cousin, if that's OK.'

Goliath looked hurt.

Limpy shrugged.

If that's what the ancient human wanted, fair enough. He'd been very to kind to them, so it seemed ungrateful to argue.

All Limpy could think about as he peed into the pot was finding Charm.

The ancient human's map was spot on.

Limpy and Goliath followed the path to the frangipani bush he'd described, turned left, were chased all the way to the giant fungus by a hungry crab, turned right, found the tree with the orange moss growing on it, turned right again, followed the slime trail of a giant slug who tried to suck their eyes out, took the left fork at the bat skull, meandered through the forest while Goliath went after a flying beetle for lunch and then spat it out when it tried to eat his tongue, turned left again at a big rubber tree where Goliath filled his mouth to bursting with Amazon bubblegum, hopped for ages keeping an eye out for bloodsucking bats, and suddenly there she was, standing on the river bank next to where Limpy had dug the grave for her necklace.

Charm.

Limpy was about to yell her name and rush over

and fling his arms around her when he saw something that hadn't been on the ancient human's map.

Flatface, standing close to Charm, speaking to her in a very unpleasant voice.

'Call yourself a toad?' he was saying. 'I've seen bigger pimples on a monkey's bum.'

'Go away,' said Charm.

'You're the most pathetic little runt I've ever seen,' jeered Flatface. 'I bet boys run a mile when they see you. They probably think you're a toenail that's fallen off a sloth.'

'I'm not listening,' said Charm.

'What?' said Flatface. 'Don't you like me calling you names? You'd better spray me then, hadn't you. Come on, midget-features, squirt me with your poison. Squirt me, squirt me, squirt me, I dare you.'

Flatface started dancing around Charm, poking his tongue out at her.

As Limpy hurried closer, he saw to his horror that Flatface had the leaf parcel. He was holding it up so that if Charm squirted him, she'd hit the parcel and give Flatface the missing ingredient he was desperate for.

Limpy was about to yell to Charm not to fire, but before he could, she started squirting.

Not at Flatface, though. Charm aimed her ribbons of poison out over the river where they fell harmlessly into the water.

Flatface was as stunned by this as Limpy.

He stared at the watery ripples, then his face crumpled.

'This is hopeless,' he wailed. 'I give up.'

He threw the leaf parcel onto the ground, turned, and stamped dejectedly away.

Limpy rushed over to Charm.

'Are you OK?' he said.

She stared at him, eyes widening with relief and joy.

'Limpy, Goliath, thank swamp,' she said. 'When I heard you were here I panicked. I thought I'd never find you.'

'We came to rescue you,' said Goliath.

Limpy saw Charm frown and open her mouth to tell them both that she didn't need to be rescued, then her face softened and she gave them a big hug instead.

Limpy glowed with love for her.

He remembered the horrible things Flatface had called her.

'Flatface didn't mean those things,' Limpy whispered to Charm. 'He just wanted your poison pus for his war plans.'

Charm thought about this.

'I reckoned the poor bloke was just crotchety because of what the humans did to his head,' she said. 'I'd be pretty ratty if I had a face that shape. Didn't seem fair to squirt him. But he was getting on my nerves so I thought I'd better empty my poison sacs before I got tempted to let him have it.'

Limpy gazed at Charm. He'd never felt prouder to have her as a sister.

Goliath was staring at Charm in disbelief.

'So you ditched your ammo in the river?' he said.

'That's right,' said Limpy, giving Goliath a stern look. 'I think that makes Charm a war hero.'

Charm looked thoughtful.

'I've been watching the creatures around here,' she said. 'How they do awful things to each other all the time. And do you know what I've realised? They can't help it. No matter what they want, food, self-defence, a bigger backyard, they use violence. Their world's a jungle. Snakes, spiders, blood-sucking bats, killer wasps, humans, they're all the same. Only cane toads are different because we can choose not to be violent.'

Limpy's warts tingled with pride as he looked at his dear, clever sister.

'Is that ancient wisdom?' he asked.

'No,' said Charm. 'I only realised it this morning.'

'Yeah, well tomorrow morning,' said Goliath, 'you'll realise it's wombat poo. What if cane toads want to be violent?'

Before Charm could reply, Limpy heard a desperate croak in the distance. The croak of a cane toad in distress.

Limpy spun round.

Through the trees he could see Flatface struggling in a net. The net was in the hands of a human.

Limpy peered harder. He recognised the human. It was the pilot from the small plane they'd arrived on.

As the pilot carried the net further into the forest, Flatface's cries were getting fainter.

'Help me. Somebody help me, please.'

'Come on,' said Limpy to Charm and Goliath. 'He mightn't be the nicest bloke around, but we can't just let him be kidnapped.'

They set off after the human.

26

By the time Limpy, Goliath and Charm caught up with the human, he was loading Flatface into the small plane.

'Oh, no,' said Charm. 'This isn't going to be easy.'

Limpy saw what she meant. Flatface was already in a cage.

'Come on,' said Limpy. 'We've got to try.'

They hopped across the dry grass of the landing strip. Limpy was used to being the slowest because of his crook leg, but for some reason today Goliath was lagging behind. Limpy could hear him puffing and wheezing.

Limpy glanced over his shoulder and saw why.

Goliath's mouth was bulging with a huge amount of Amazon bubblegum.

Before Limpy could suggest Goliath ditch some of his load, they reached the plane. Limpy pulled the others into the shadow of the fuselage, well away from the pilot who was tinkering with one of the engines.

The cargo door was still open. Limpy peered in and what he saw made him forget bubblegum completely.

The plane was full of wooden cages, each one with a cane toad in it.

'Stack me,' croaked Limpy.

'It's a mass kidnapping,' said Charm.

'This,' muttered Goliath, 'is war.'

The caged toads saw Limpy and Goliath and Charm and started croaking for help. Until they were silenced by a familiar voice.

'Be quiet everyone. Do you want our friends to be captured as well?'

Limpy saw it was Raoul, gripping the bars of his cage, head bruised and warts bleeding.

'We've got to move fast,' said Limpy to Goliath and Charm. 'We've got to get them out before the plane takes off.'

Luckily there were rivets on the side of the plane, and rust, which gave Limpy and the others something to grip with their toes and fingers. They clambered into the plane.

Limpy saw that the cages were held shut with twisted pieces of wire.

He grabbed a spanner from an open toolbox and tried to prise the twist of wire off Raoul's cage door. It was no good, he wasn't strong enough.

'Let me,' said Goliath. 'I've straightened out lizard's intestines that are tougher than this.'

Goliath jammed the spanner behind the wire and pulled until his eyeballs and warts bulged.

Suddenly the wire gave and the cage door swung open.

Raoul stepped out and embraced Goliath.

'Our ancient legends tell of a hero,' said Raoul. 'A hero who will one day come from afar to save us. Now I know he has arrived.'

Goliath blushed. 'Don't forget Limpy and Charm,' he said. 'They're my assistants.'

Limpy was about to suggest that they all get to work on all the other cages, but before he could the whole plane started vibrating.

'It's the engines,' yelled Charm from the doorway.

Limpy could hear the roar getting louder.

'Quick,' he yelled. 'Let's get these other cages open.'

They grabbed more tools and worked on three more cages, Charm and Limpy using a spanner together. But before they could get them open, the plane lurched forward and they were flung back in a heap.

'The plane's taking off,' said Charm after she'd moved Goliath's knee out of her mouth. 'It's too late.'

'The pilot's left the cargo door open,' said Goliath. 'Why's he taking off with the door open?'

'Probably so we don't suffocate,' said Raoul. 'Wherever he's taking us, they want us alive.'

All the cane toads fell silent. Limpy could see

they were each imagining what kind of awful place that might be.

Then Limpy had an idea.

'Goliath,' he said. 'Spit out your bubblegum.'

Goliath stopped chewing and glared at Limpy. 'All our lives are in danger,' he said, 'and you're worried about a bit of bubblegum?'

'Spit it out and give it to me,' said Limpy. 'I've thought of a way to get our friends back on the ground.'

Raoul stood in the doorway of the plane, wind whipping across his noble face. He embraced Goliath, then Charm, then Limpy.

'You are all heroes,' he said. 'May you fulfill your quest and live long and happy lives.'

'Thanks,' said Goliath. 'Hope the scabs heal.'

Raoul gave the bubblegum in his mouth a final chew, then jumped.

Limpy peered anxiously down at Raoul's plummeting figure. He hoped Goliath's bubble-blowing lesson had been clear enough. And that Raoul had enough gum in his mouth.

Suddenly a large bubble erupted over Raoul's head and his plummet slowed to a float.

'It's working,' said Charm, gazing down, amazed and delighted.

The other cane toads, all crowding around the doorway and all chewing enthusiastically, broke into applause.

'I told you dividing my mouthful of bubblegum among this lot would give them enough each,' said Goliath. 'I've got a big mouth.'

Limpy didn't argue with that.

Now Raoul had showed that Limpy's idea would work, all the other cane toads clamoured to be next.

'Form a line, troops,' ordered Goliath. 'No pushing and that's an order.'

One by one the other cane toads jumped and floated down towards the forest, each under a big rubbery bubble.

'I hope they survive the biting ants at the top of the trees,' said Limpy.

'No worries,' said Goliath. 'We did and we're not even locals.'

The last to jump was Flatface.

Just before he did, he turned to Limpy.

'Bulldozers don't understand what peace is,' said Flatface. 'To make them listen, you'll need something stronger than friendship.'

Limpy didn't know what to say.

Flatface turned to Charm. 'Sorry I called you all those names,' he said. 'Actually, you're quite good-looking.'

Limpy could see Charm didn't know what to say either.

Goliath stepped forward. 'Limpy's Mum reckons I'm quite good-looking too,' he said. 'When I don't dribble.'

Flatface jumped.

'Our turn,' said Goliath, looking around for the last bits of bubblegum.

Limpy and Charm glanced at each other. They'd been dreading breaking this next bit of news to Goliath.

'Sorry Goliath,' said Limpy. 'I'm afraid there's none left for us.'

He put his arm round Goliath's big middle and waited for his cousin's anger to turn to tears, which it usually did when all their lives were in danger.

While Limpy was waiting, Charm tapped him urgently on the shoulder.

'Limpy,' she whispered. 'Does this plane have automatic pilot?'

Limpy remembered that a pelican had explained to him once about automatic pilot. It was what pelicans used when they were filleting a salmon in mid-flight.

'I don't know,' said Limpy. 'Why?'

'Well,' said Charm, her voice wobbling. 'I was just wondering which was going to happen first. Us being captured or us crashing.'

Limpy looked up.

The pilot, surrounded by empty cages, was glaring down at them, furious.

'I think being captured,' said Limpy as the pilot picked all three of them up, flung them into the toolbox and slammed the lid.

27

The plane didn't crash.

'Must have automatic pilot,' whispered Limpy in the dark.

'This toolbox smells,' said Goliath. 'And these washers taste stale.'

'Limpy,' whispered Charm. 'Where do you think this plane's going?'

'Don't know,' said Limpy.

He hoped it was Los Angeles because at least they could get a plane back to Australia from there. Except the pilot hadn't looked like he wanted to help them get home.

Limpy reached out in the darkness and gave Charm a hug.

He didn't know what else to say. He also didn't know what to say if Charm asked him about the ancient secret.

How can I tell her, thought Limpy miserably. We've travelled all this way. We've been through so much. How can I tell Charm that I forgot to ask the ancient human the secret of living in peace with other humans?

OK, he'd had an excuse. He'd been over-whelmed at discovering Charm was alive. He'd been desperate to find her. But he'd still forgotten to ask.

How could I, thought Limpy. How could I forget the whole point of our quest?

He didn't have an answer, so he sat in silence. For a long time he heard nothing but the distant hum of the engines.

Then a long groan echoed around the toolbox.

'Are you two OK?' asked Limpy, anxious that Charm or Goliath might be ill.

'It's Goliath,' said Charm. 'I think those washers he ate are disagreeing with him.'

Goliath gave another groan. 'It's not the washers,' he said. 'I've just remembered something. I left an order with my troops at home. If we're not back by the new moon, I told them to assume we've been killed by humans and to go on a revenge mission.'

Limpy's insides dropped even though there was no air turbulence outside the plane.

'What sort of revenge mission?' he asked.

'I ordered them to scratch all the cars in the human suburb,' said Goliath.

Limpy's insides crashed and burned.

'That's terrible,' he croaked.

'I know,' said Goliath. 'I completely forgot to tell them to let all the tyres down as well.'

For the rest of the flight, Limpy could only think about one thing. He was still thinking about it as the plane landed and he felt the toolbox being loaded into a vehicle and driven somewhere.

One awful thing.

The huge merciless war Limpy knew humans would wage against anyone who scratched their cars.

28

When the toolbox lid was finally flung open, Limpy saw to his horror that it had already started.

The global war between humans and cane toads.

He and Charm and Goliath staggered out of the toolbox into a nightmare.

Fireballs were exploding in a dark sky. The night air was full of smoke and stench. Humans in ragged military uniforms were clambering over piles of rubble, aiming huge guns. And all around, slumped and bleeding and pitiful, were dead cane toads.

Limpy could hardly take it all in. He was dimly aware of Charm whimpering and clutching on to him.

They both ducked as a burly helmeted human, chest criss-crossed with belts of bullets, dragged himself out of a crater, heaved a machine gun onto his shoulder and blasted several cane toads into tiny pieces.

'What's going on?' yelled Goliath into Limpy's ear.

He looked as stunned as Limpy felt.

'War,' said Limpy, feeling faint. 'World war.'

Goliath glared up at the human with the smoking gun. 'You mongrel,' he yelled and flung himself at the towering figure.

'No,' screamed Limpy, but it was too late.

Goliath landed on the human's boot. The human shook him off, then pointed the machine gun at Goliath's head.

Limpy and Charm held onto each other in helpless terror and watched as Goliath stared up at the gun.

'Goliath,' yelled Charm. 'Hop for it.'

Limpy saw that Goliath couldn't move because the human soldier was treading on his leg.

Charm was already squirting at the human and Limpy did too. But the human's helmet had a perspex visor and their poison pus just sprayed harmlessly against it.

Limpy saw the human taking aim.

Goliath started blubbering. 'Please,' he begged the human. 'Don't shoot. I'll disband my army. I'll give up wavy mud. Please.'

Limpy tried to throw himself forward, to drag Goliath away, but Charm held him back.

'Don't,' she sobbed. 'It's suicide.'

Limpy saw the human's finger starting to squeeze the trigger.

'No,' screamed an anguished voice, and Limpy wasn't sure if it was Goliath or him or both.

Then suddenly night turned into day and the explosions stopped and somebody wheeled a tea trolley onto the battlefield.

Limpy blinked, stunned.

He looked up. High above, massive lights hung from the ceiling of what Limpy realised was a vast room, even bigger than the supermarket and the airport.

The human with the gun had flipped up his visor and was picking up a very wobbly Goliath.

'Hi there,' said the human to Goliath. 'I see the live ones have arrived.'

Limpy didn't understand the words, but what he hoped the human was saying was 'we surrender, we surrender, all we want is to live in peace and friendship with cane toads for ever.'

It was possible. The human was stroking the stunned and bug-eyed Goliath in a friendly way.

'What's going on?' croaked Charm.

'Not sure,' said Limpy. He decided to ask a local. He saw one close by, a cane toad sitting on a pile of rubble.

'Excuse me,' said Limpy. 'What's going on?'

The cane toad didn't answer. Limpy asked again, and when the cane toad didn't answer again, he decided the cane toad must either be dead or shell-shocked. He'd seen shell-shocked crabs like this after humans had thrown shells at them.

Then he looked closer and saw that the cane toad was made of cloth with plastic eyes.

I don't get this, thought Limpy. Perhaps it's me who's either dead or shell-shocked.

'You wanna know what's going on?' said a voice behind him. 'Lunch, that's what's going on.'

Limpy turned round.

A cane toad munching a grasshopper in a bun was pointing to a big food trolley next to the tea trolley.

'Lunch?' said Limpy.

'Shooting has stopped for lunch,' said the toad, who Limpy could now see wasn't a real cane toad, just a smooth-skinned frog with makeup and fake warts.

'Shooting has stopped for lunch?' said Limpy. He had no idea that wars stopped for lunch.

'Jeez,' said the frog, rolling his eyes. 'Wake up and smell the coffee. Unless you want to be an extra for the rest of your life. We get a meal break every two hours. It's in the contract.'

'Contract?' said Limpy.

'That wad of paper your agent looks after for you,' said the frog, shaking his head. 'The one you did a mud-print on to be in this movie. The one with *Armageddon 4 – Rise Of The Toads* on the front.'

Limpy digested this.

A movie. He'd seen movies on the big outdoor screen at the campsite back home. But never with cane toads in them.

'Hey Limpy,' called Goliath.

For a moment, Limpy couldn't see him.

'He's over there,' said Charm, pointing.

Limpy saw that the human who'd been holding Goliath was sitting in a canvas chair surrounded by other humans. They were dabbing his face and hair with little brushes. Goliath was sitting on his knee, being dabbed with little brushes too.

'This bloke here's the star of the movie,' said Goliath grinning. 'I think he's gunna make me a star too.'

'No chance,' muttered the frog. 'We toads never get top billing. We're just props. This movie was gonna be *Armageddon 4 – Rise Of The Worms* until the producer got the idea of using toads. Apparently he saw a movie with a scary toad in it on a flight back from Australia.'

Limpy remembered Goliath's shadow on the aircraft movie screen.

He decided it was best not to say anything.

'I like Hollywood,' said Goliath as a human dabbed makeup onto his warts. 'Can we stay here and be in lots of war movies?'

Limpy and Charm looked at each other.

'No,' said Charm. 'Absolutely not.'

'By my calculation,' said Limpy, 'full moon at

home is in six days. If we're not back by then, a real war will break out, remember?'

Goliath's shoulders slumped.

'Oh yeah,' he said. 'I forgot.'

29

The stretch limo pulled up at the airport and Goliath hopped out onto the red carpet.

Limpy and Charm hurried after him.

Cameras flashed and a crowd of humans with microphones and notepads craned forward for a closer look.

'No interviews,' said Goliath, turning his best warts to the cameras. 'Just autographs if you've got some mud.'

Limpy thought about strangling Goliath. He decided not to because he didn't want Mum and Dad seeing a picture of it in the paper.

'Goliath,' hissed Charm. 'Behave yourself. This isn't for you. It's for him.'

She pointed up at the star of the movie, who was stepping out of the limo and smiling at the cameras.

'It's for us too,' said Goliath sulkily. 'We're stars too.'

'No we're not,' said Limpy. 'We're here to create a photo operation.'

The smooth-skinned frog, who'd followed them out of the limo, rolled his eyes. 'Photo opportunity,' he said wearily, as the star picked him up. 'The word is photo opportunity. A B-grade movie actor flying back to his ranch isn't news, so they've brought us along to beef up the publicity angle.'

'That's right,' said Limpy to Goliath, even though he hadn't understood everything the frog had just said. 'And it's great for us because this is the airport where we can get a plane back to Australia.'

'I think we should sneak away now,' said Charm. 'While the humans are taking photos of the star holding the frog.'

'Hang on,' said Goliath. 'I think they want me in the photo with them.'

'No we don't,' said the frog. 'Trust me, honey.'

Before Goliath could argue, Limpy and Charm dragged him under a soft-drink machine.

Limpy peeped out at the crowd. Nobody had seen them go.

'Hey, beautiful,' yelled a voice. 'I love you. You're a star.'

Almost nobody.

Limpy saw where the voice was coming from. A familiar figure was in the crowd, jumping up between human feet, waving at Charm.

A dust mite.

'Oh, no,' muttered Charm. 'It's Myron.'

'Thank you,' said Goliath, blushing and waving back to Myron. 'You're too kind.'

Once they were on the plane to Australia, and safely strapped under three empty seats next to the rolled-up plastic things, and the plane had taken off, Limpy was finally able to relax.

And get depressed.

During the past few days he'd been so busy worrying about how to get off the movie set and back to Australia, he hadn't had time to even think about the much bigger problem.

The total failure of their quest.

His failure.

I can't put it off any longer, thought Limpy miserably. I've got to tell the others.

'Charm and Goliath,' he said. 'I've got something to confess.'

'What,' said Goliath. 'That you should have let me stay and talk to my fan the dust mite?'

'No,' said Limpy. 'Not that.'

He took a deep breath.

But it was no good.

He couldn't do it.

He didn't manage to do it until they'd landed in Australia and found some birds to take them on the last part of the journey and they were almost home.

Limpy looked across at Charm and Goliath, dozing in the warm slipstream underneath their birds.

'Charm and Goliath,' he said. 'I've got something to tell you.'

They both opened their eyes and looked at him.

Limpy took a big sad breath.

'I failed in the quest,' he said. 'When we visited the ancient human, I forgot to ask him the secret of living in peace with other humans.'

Limpy waited miserably for them to respond.

'That's OK,' said Charm softly. 'I asked him.'

Limpy stared at her, his heart going faster than a hummingbird's armpit.

'What did he say?' croaked Limpy.

Charm opened her mouth to tell him, then glanced across at Goliath, who was listening with interest.

'I'll tell you when we get back home,' she said.

Limpy woke up. It felt good to be back in his own room. Plus he was still glowing from the welcome home party. All those hugs long into the night under the almost-full moon.

Then Limpy remembered that Charm still hadn't told him what the ancient human had said.

He hopped out of bed, gave the rellies a quick dust, washed his tongue in the swamp, admired the sunrise and went looking for the others.

He couldn't find them anywhere.

Not Charm, Goliath, Mum or Dad.

That's strange, thought Limpy. I didn't sleep longer than usual. I haven't been eating the pills humans sometimes chuck out of passing cars, so I wasn't in a coma.

He tried to remember if today was a special day. Mum's birthday, or the day each week they took Goliath to the echidna nest to clean his teeth on the bristles.

No, neither of those.

Then Limpy noticed something very odd. The swamp was almost deserted. Not a cane toad to be seen.

Panic gripped Limpy's throat sac.

Had human picnickers come while he was asleep and attacked the swamp? Was everyone dead?

Limpy looked around wildly.

That couldn't be it. None of the bushes or swamp grass or reeds were even a tiny bit bruised. Humans on a violent rampage would have crushed them. And left behind empty drink cans and supermarket bags.

Limpy felt dizzy with relief.

But it was still very strange.

The only living creature he could see was an ant dragging a ball of wombat poo along a bush path.

'G'day,' said the ant. 'Why aren't you at the picnic?'

'What picnic?' said Limpy.

'The picnic,' said the ant, pointing along the bush path. 'The picnic all the others have gone to. The human picnic.'

Limpy found the human picnic in a bush clearing.

The adult and kid humans were playing ball at one end of the clearing, and their picnic rug, covered in food and drinks, was at the other.

All the cane toads were crouched in the long grass, looking at the picnic rug expectantly.

'Ah, there you are, love,' said Mum, giving Limpy a squeeze. 'You looked so tired and jet-lagged we didn't want to wake you.'

'You deserved a sleep-in after a heroic journey like yours,' said Dad. He turned to Charm. 'Can we start now, love?'

Charm nodded. She gave Limpy a quick hug. 'I wouldn't have started without you,' she said.

'Which is why we've been waiting half the morning,' grumbled Goliath.

This is it, thought Limpy. Charm's going to reveal the secret of living in peace and friendship with humans.

He was all ears.

But instead of talking, Charm hopped over to the picnic rug and did a quick pee in each of the drinks.

Limpy couldn't believe what he was seeing. 'Stop,' he yelled at her. 'That's not the way to do it.'

'I agree,' said Goliath. 'I'd put in about twice as much.'

Charm hopped back over, breathless and excited.

'Why did you do that?' said Limpy, stunned.

Charm gave him a patient smile. 'Remember when you visited the ancient human,' she said. 'How he asked you to pee in the water pot?'

'Yes,' said Limpy, puzzled.

'That's because,' said Charm, 'many generations ago, one of the ancient human's ancestors made a wonderful discovery. If a human, every new moon, drinks a tiny drop of cane toad urine, that human will be blessed with a long and healthy and happy and peaceful life.'

Limpy stared at Charm.

'That's the ancient wisdom the old human told me,' she said. 'That's how we can help humans to be happy and friendly like the people in the Amazon village.'

Limpy took this in.

He liked the sound of it.

'But,' said Charm, 'the pee must only come from a cane toad who feels warm and friendly towards humans. Which is why you and I can do it but Goliath can't yet.'

'I feel warm towards the mongrels,' muttered Goliath. 'Honest.'

'Be patient, love,' said Mum, giving Goliath a squeeze. 'You'll get there.'

Limpy put his arms round Charm and gave her a huge hug, his warts tingling with love and gratitude.

'Thank you,' he said.

'It was a difficult and dangerous quest,' said Dad. 'You all deserve our thanks.'

'Including me,' said Goliath.

Already Limpy was imagining the suburbs of Australia full of cane toads doing their bit to help humans become healthier and happier and less interested in violence and killing.

Brave noble cane toads sidling unseen up to cups and mugs and glasses and bottles and peeing in them.

'Well,' said Mum. 'What do you think?'

'Worth a try?' said Dad.

'I think it's definitely worth a try,' said Limpy.

His eyes met Charm's and Goliath's, and he could see they did too.

Limpy smiled happily.

With a sister like Charm and a cousin like Goliath, anything was possible.

About the Author

Morris Gleitzman grew up in England and came to Australia when he was sixteen. He was a frozen-chicken thawer, sugar-mill rolling-stock unhooker, fashion-industry trainee, student, department-store Santa, TV producer, newspaper columnist and screenwriter. Then he had a wonderful experience. He wrote a novel for young people. Now he's a children's author. *Toad Away* is his twentieth book.

Visit Morris at his website:
www.morrisgleitzman.com

Boy Overboard

A story of adventure, ball control and hope.

Jamal and Bibi have a dream.
To lead Australia to soccer glory in
the next World Cup.

But first they must face landmines,
pirates, storms and assassins.

Can Jamal and his family survive their
incredible journey and get to Australia?

Sometimes, to save the people you love,
you have to go overboard.

Adults Only

The kitchen was a mess. Packets and jars had been flung around. Half the stuff in the fridge was on the floor. There was a trail of flour running along the passage.

For a second Jake thought one of the magazine people must have had an urge to make a cake and decided to do it in their room.

Or was someone else in the house?

Jake's an only kid.
He's the only kid in his family.
He's the only kid on his island.

Or that's what he thinks . . .

A funny and surprising story about
new and old friends.

Bumface!

Bumface!
That's who Angus wants to be.
He dreams of being bold, brave, wild and free.
Like the pirate in the stories he tells his
younger brother and sister.

Instead Angus is just plain tired from changing
nappies and wiping food off walls.

His mum calls him Mr Dependable, but Angus
can barely cope. Another baby would be a disaster.
So Angus comes up with a bold and brave plan
to stop her getting pregnant.

That's when he meets Rindi. And Angus
thought *he* had problems . . .

Wicked!

Paul Jennings and Morris Gleitzman
A NOVEL IN SIX PARTS
It'll suck you in!

Something very weird is happening to Dawn and Rory.
Slurping slobberers want to suck their bones out.
Strange steel sheep want to smash them to pieces.
Giant frogs want to crunch them up. Their parents
can't help them. Dawn and Rory are on their own.

It's wild. It's wacky. It's WICKED!

Deadly!

Morris Gleitzman and Paul Jennings
A NOVEL IN SIX PARTS
You could die laughing!

Join Amy and Sprocket as they desperately search
for their families – a quest that will take them to the
weirdest nudist colony in the world. Uncovering
deadly secret after deadly secret, Amy and Sprocket
are lured deeper into a mystery that grows more
exciting with every turn of the page.

second childhood

'Smalley,' said Mr Cruickshank, 'do you
know what you're going to end up as?'
'Sheep's poop, sir,' whispered Mark.
Mr Cruickshank looked startled. 'I wouldn't
have put it quite like that.'

It looks like Mark's heading for oblivion.
Until he and his friends discover they've lived
before. Not only that – they were Famous and
Important People!

The Other Facts of Life

'Comfortable?' asked the shoe shop assistant.
'With forty thousand kids starving to death
every day?' said Ben. 'Are you?'

Ben's dad has told him the facts of life.
But it's the other facts that are worrying Ben
and he decides to find out his own answers.
He's deadly serious – and the results
are very, very funny.

misery guts

What does a kid do when his mum
and dad are misery guts?
Move them to a tropical paradise, decides Keith.
That'll cheer them up.
It's a brilliant plan – if he can pull it off.

worry warts

What does a kid do when his mum
and dad are worry warts?
Make them rich, decides Keith. Very, very rich.
It's a brilliant plan – if it works.

puppy fat

What does a kid do when his mum
and dad are past it?
Get them into shape, decides Keith.
And find them new partners.
It's a brilliant plan – but he'll need help.